Red Nation
Blue Nation

Larry & Ann Nunnally

Love and
Blessings
Ann Nunnally

TRILOGY CHRISTIAN PUBLISHERS

TUSTIN, CA

Trilogy Christian Publishers
A Wholly Owned Subsidiary of Trinity Broadcasting Network
2442 Michelle Drive
Tustin, CA 92780

Red Nation Blue Nation

Rights Department, 2442 Michelle Drive, Tustin, CA 92780.

Trilogy Christian Publishing/TBN and colophon are trademarks of Trinity Broadcasting Network.

For information about special discounts for bulk purchases, please contact Trilogy Christian Publishing.

Trilogy Disclaimer: The views and content expressed in this book are those of the author and may not necessarily reflect the views and doctrine of Trilogy Christian Publishing or the Trinity Broadcasting Network.

Manufactured in the United States of America

10 9 8 7 6 5 4 3 2 1

Library of Congress Cataloging-in-Publication Data is available.

ISBN: 978-1-68556-713-2

E-ISBN: 978-1-68556-714-9

Contents

Introduction

The United States of America has not been as divided politically, emotionally, and philosophically since the Civil War. We have always had disagreements and seen things differently but were able to come together during crisis times. Not anymore. Wars, natural disasters, and even a worldwide pandemic have not spurred us on to embrace one another as Americans. Rather, we have broken up into splinter groups and fostered a huge level of distrust. The anger in our country has led to harsh incivility that punctuates our society.

The sharpest division is between the conservative and liberal camps. Each state is even identified as Red (conservative) or Blue (liberal). The two major political parties refuse to work together and have resorted to name-calling, threats, and a "gotcha" mentality.

This book is about an amazing "fix" for this situation that could actually happen in the not-so-distant future. What if the United States of America was *dissolved* and two cyber nations were created to represent each of the two main political ideologies of the American people. Imagine a Red Nation and a Blue Nation that were digitally superimposed on the land we call the United States of America. No one would migrate to different areas of the country to be with like-minded people, but rather each new nation would be connected by a vast computer network. The Red Nation could live out its conservative laws, tax rates, business practices, and religious ideals, while the Blue Nation would do the same thing but in a progressive manner.

The state governments wouldn't change, only the federal government. Now, there would be *two* federal governments working with the states to provide goods and services desired by the conservative or Red Nation and the liberal or Blue Nation. After all, a nation is the people, not the land the people live on.

Think about it—no need to compromise with the "idiots" that are damaging the country. You would have your own country, and the "idiots" would have their country. Obviously, there would be questions about how to furnish infrastructure, military protection, law enforcement, and court systems for each individual nation. Well, remember, this all takes place in the future, and those problems could be solved by former governmental organizations becoming non-profit corporations that basically "rented" roads, military protection, and social services to each new nation.

So, there you have it. *Red Nation Blue Nation.* Enjoy the story of the most amazing social experiment in the history of the world.

CHAPTER 1

Red Nation
Blue Nation

"Mr. President! Mr. President! Wake up, Mr. President!" said Chief of Staff George Turner excitedly. "Mr. President, you must wake up! It's an emergency, Mr. President!" whined George.

The president slightly rolled over and squinted as the soft light from the hallway pierced the darkness of his dreams. It had been a late night with friends celebrating the release of unemployment numbers. He had reveled a little too much with his favorite scotch, and now he was being awakened by a hysterical chief of staff.

"George, have you gone mad? It's 3:30 a.m.! This had better be good," President Watson barked wearily as he tried to sound stern.

"Just turn on your holovision, Mr. President, and see for yourself!" said the exasperated Turner.

President Kennedy Watson sat up and rubbed his eyes sleepily before saying, "Holo on!" The holovision whirred to life as the array of ceiling and floor projectors meshed with the five surround sound speakers to display a bright full-color HD rumbling mushroom cloud in the middle of the president's bedroom.

"My God..." whispered President Watson as the news reporter rambled on about the nuclear bomb that had been detonated on an uninhabited island in the middle of the Atlantic. The bomb had been a rather small one for a nuclear weapon, only about twenty kilotons, or roughly the size of the Fat Man bomb that was dropped on Nagasaki in 1945.

"Mr. President, the person responsible for this outrage has contacted the Pentagon and said he would like to speak with you and your cabinet by holo-conference at 8 a.m. sharp," said Turner.

President Watson was trembling. How could this happen? The Nuclear Defense Alignment Treaty of 2038 assured that no nuclear device could be detonated before the orbiting space-based laser system destroyed the carrier missile. Russia, China, England, Pakistan, and every other country that had acquired nuclear weapons had worked together to design, build, and launch the NDAT system. No nuclear devices had been detonated since tactical weapons were deployed in the Jihadist Coalition War of 2029. There was much to be explained. Kennedy knew he wouldn't sleep anymore tonight, so he plodded toward the mini kitchen in search of a strong cup of coffee. The kitchen staff had already been alerted, and the president could smell the rich Colombian brew as he walked into the mini kitchen and plopped down at the small table.

President Kennedy Watson, a lifelong lawyer and Democrat senator from New Jersey, had been named after President John Fitzgerald Kennedy. Kennedy's grandfather had been one of JFK's golf buddies and confidants, so naming Kennedy after JFK had been a natural choice for the Watson clan.

K. W., as Watson's close friends called him, had not been a particularly bright student in undergrad or law school, but his Harvard law degree was still an eye-opener for people on the Washington political scene. Now, as president of the United States, Watson was in his second term of what was usually described, even by his own party, as a mediocre presidency. The economy was steady, and the U. S. wasn't involved in any major conflicts in the world. Mediocre was certainly better than tragic. President Watson sat alone with his thoughts and downed three cups of coffee until time to get dressed. He had already asked George to alert his entire cabinet to meet him in the West Wing Situation Room at 7:50 a.m. He walked back to the bedroom where Pierre, his valet, had already laid out his dark navy suit and bright red tie. The president liked to wear power colors like red, black, and navy. He thought these colors looked good with his crown of graying red hair and made him look more presidential.

President Watson and his full cabinet assembled in the "war" room next to the oval office in the West Wing of the White House. The joint chiefs had been rushed in by jet-copter to join the gathering. Each seat was equipped with a holovision that could project video mail (or Vmail) images in real-time. President Watson looked at the dewy roses outside the large plate glass windows and sighed. This second term of office was going so well...and now this. As the staff assembled, Kennedy Watson thought about his public service career. Kennedy was well-schooled in politics and well-liked. He had practiced law for a few years before he was elected to the House of Representatives at the age of thirty-one. After serving three terms as a U. S. Congressional Representative from New Jersey, Watson had moved on to the Senate for eighteen years. He was elected to the presidency at the age of fifty-eight. Watson's thoughts were broken when he heard his chief of staff call the meeting to order.

The holovision came to life promptly at 8 a.m. and displayed the real-time 3D image of a smallish gray-haired man behind a huge mahogany desk with an American flag and a brass cross in the background. The entire cabinet let out groans and gasps as they recognized the figure. It was Clark Johnson, evangelical megachurch preacher and conservative activist. Johnson had been one of President Watson's greatest critics and had crafted a brand of Christian Nationalism that was scoffed at by most "thinking people" but enjoyed huge success in conservative circles. Johnson's political organization had endorsed several relatively unknown candidates in the last election that had slightly bolstered the slim Republican hold on the House of Representatives. The Senate was still in the hands of the Democrats, so Watson had muddled along with no real agenda. Clark Johnson's political theatrics had done little to "upset the apple cart" in Washington, D. C.

A wry smile spread across Clark Johnson's face as the preacher began to speak.

"Hello, President Watson, or should I say, ex-President Watson! How did you like my handiwork in the Atlantic?" said Clark Johnson with a happy-sounding Southern drawl.

"You!" snarled Watson. "How could you have had *anything* to do with that nuke in the ocean? You're just a meddling Texas preacher, for God's sake!"

"I might be a meddling Texas preacher, but I'm now the head of this republic, former President Watson."

"Quit calling me former president, you idiot! I *am* the president!"

"Not anymore, you're not!" said Reverend Johnson in an attempt to imitate Watson's voice. "You see, ex-

President Watson, not only did my people detonate that nuke in the Atlantic, but we have three more nuclear devices hidden in three of America's major cities that I will most surely activate if you and your cronies don't do exactly as I say."

"That's impossible!" screamed Watson. "How did you get a nuclear bomb anyway?"

"Oh, it wasn't too hard. Why don't you ask Admiral Choi?" said Clark Johnson in his well-known Southern twang.

Admiral Nancy Choi was the head of the joint chiefs. She was the first Asian American to hold that high rank and one of the most popular women in America. Choi had planned the final invasion that broke the back of the Jihadist forces during the war fought in 2029. Nancy Choi's amazing rise from Navy SEAL commander to admiral had been the stuff of legends. Choi's skillfulness in tactical warfare was unparalleled, and she was incredibly popular with the American public.

All eyes turned to Admiral Choi as she spoke, "He's exactly right, K. W. I not only procured the weapon from a stash of old ISIS armaments in Pakistan, but my forces deployed and detonated it for the whole world to see. Your reign of political misery is over. You and your pack of pathetic government parasites have done nothing but tangle this country in political red tape. Pack your bags and get out! And take your sorry do-nothing cabinet with you! Brother Clark is in charge now."

Watson was frozen, speechless, lost.

Clark began to speak, "That's right, Mr. Ex-President. Brother Clark is in charge now."

George Turner spoke up through tears, "But why? This is all madness. What is this all about?"

"It's about the greatest social experiment ever known to mankind, Mr. Turner. This country has been divided into two camps for so long that the will of the people is ignored as you ridiculous politicians try to force your ever-evolving ideologies on the masses. Well, that stops today, and this is how we will proceed," stated Clark firmly.

The shocked but silent cabinet members listened intently as Clark Johnson explained the social experiment that would change the lives of Americans forever.

"Since the country is so bitterly divided into either conservative or progressive ideological camps, we are simply going to give the people want they want—a country unencumbered by dealing with their political foes. Because of the Every American Connected Act (or EACA) of 2027, we have already made technical arrangements to have two separate governments occupy the same soil. The whole transition will be accomplished online. We will develop a Conservative, Red Nation, and a Liberal, Blue Nation. Here is how this new system of governments will work:

1. "Each U. S. citizen has three months to choose the Red Nation or the Blue Nation. If they refuse to choose a country, one will be assigned to them based on their party affiliation or voting record—yes, I know the federal government illegally catalogs voting records. If people refuse to cooperate, they will be jailed for the duration of this political experiment. Corporations and other businesses will also choose a nation based on decisions made by owners and/or stockholders.

2. "During this three-month period, the basic tenets of conservatism and liberalism will be explained through news media and online so each citizen can make an informed decision.

3. "During this adjustment period, martial law will be instituted by Admiral Choi and the joint chiefs to ensure order. The local, state, and federal law enforcement agencies will work with the military to keep order during the transition.

4. "The current president, his cabinet, and both legislative branches of government will be dismissed as new lawmakers will be selected for each new country within the next year.

5. "All federal, state, and local services will be delivered in a normal fashion until the new Red and Blue governments are established and go into effect.

"Just imagine—two sister countries occupying the same physical space but governing themselves without interference from the other nation. It will be delightful, amazing, and so revealing!

"I know you have questions, as do all Americans. We are releasing a Vmail of this meeting to all major news outlets, and I will address the nation tonight at 8 p.m. I suggest the rest of you clean out your desks and leave."

Kennedy Watson was livid! "What gives you the power to launch a coup?" screamed Watson! "You're a fake, a nobody—"

"Here's your answer, Kenny—the whole military command is behind us. Did you think we planned this overnight? This plan has been in the works for years as both progressive and conservative minds have hammered out the details to make these two new nations work."

Before Watson could respond, a group of armed soldiers entered the Situation Room to remove the president and his cabinet. Some of the cabinet members resisted, but most of these formerly powerful men and women willingly left with the soldiers. They were taken to their offices under guard and instructed to take their personal belongings to a staging area. From there, they would be escorted to their personal residences until all U. S. citizens were informed of the changes.

The regular White House employees were met in the various parking lots and building entrances to be detained in the White House until after Clark Johnson's message.

About 10 a.m., the news outlets received the Vmail, which included the nuclear blast segment. The public and private sectors were both shaken to the core. People walked off their jobs and drove home. Parents picked up children before the school day was half over. The markets plummeted, with the DOW losing 40 percent within thirty minutes of the announcement. Trading was suspended shortly thereafter. People began to buy up food and water, and many grocery store shelves were totally depleted. Banks were closed for fear of a run on cash, and service stations closed after all the gasoline was bought up by frightened citizens. But regardless of the near panic, Americans were in front of their holovisions or watching from a handheld device that evening at 8 p.m.

While waiting for the broadcast to begin, Clark's thoughts drifted back to his first memories of holovision development. Clark had been deeply involved in the production of his Revive America telecast and was totally intrigued by this cutting-edge mode of a more dynamic communication approach that was being developed in California. Clark had taken the time to fly to the Multi-Vision corporate headquarters in Los Angeles when holovision hardware had just begun to show promise of changing the home entertainment industry. Clark had been introduced to Manuel Alvarez, the CEO of Multi-Vision, by a mutual friend in the television production business. The two men had developed a friendship around their desire to bring the holovision concept to reality in home entertainment. Both men had been greatly influenced by the *Star Wars* films. They often laughed about the effect the scene from *A New Hope*, where R2D2 displayed the three-dimensional image of Princess Lea pleading with Obi-Wan Kenobi, had on each of them. When Clark originally saw that image at a "classic movie night" while in college, he thought, *If I was just three-dimensional like Lea, I could reach more people on an emotional level with my messages. My image could sit right in front of them and share the gospel on a personal basis.* While Manuel didn't share Clark's faith, he had certainly realized the power of three-dimensional home theater viewing. He imagined a romantic scene with lovers passionately kissing or even a bloody street fight with life-sized figures projected into a family living room. Both men knew that the results would be mind-boggling. When the two men would occasionally meet later on after holovision was a reality and installed in 70 percent of American homes, they would look each other dead in the eyes and say, "Help me, Obie-Wan Kenobi. You're my only hope!" Then they would laugh and shake hands.

Clark's remembrances were interrupted by the voice of his production manager counting down to airtime, and he quickly took a sip of water before appearing at his mahogany desk at 8 p.m. sharp. His boyish features and slim build made his fifty-two years look much younger. Without his graying hair, one might think he was barely forty years old. Clark was dressed in an open collar light blue shirt and a navy blazer. He wore his familiar combination of the American flag and cross pin on his left lapel. He smiled warmly as he began speaking in his deep Texas drawl.

"Hello, America! This is Brother Clark Johnson. Many of you have seen me on our Revive America HV program, and you know that I bear no ill will towards anyone. In fact, you will not find a person who loves America and Americans more than I do. Therefore, I have taken this bold step to simply give us all what we want—a country that fits the needs of those that are like-minded. Haven't you hated the Washington gridlock, spiraling national debt, and political posturing that goes on in our federal government? I sure have! Well, that changes today!" said Clark proudly. Clark took a sip of water and continued, "My friends and I have developed a plan to form two cyber nations. You get to choose which nation you want to be a part of—the Red Conservative Nation or the Blue Liberal Nation. You will have three months to study the basics of conservative and liberal ideologies and make your decision via NewAmerica.net at the Ameriputer in your home or business. Corporations or businesses that are taxed will make the same decision. Nonprofit organizations will defer the decisions to their individual workers. Isn't this exciting?" Clark chuckled!

"The basic operating rules for our new cyber countries will be electronically sent to all American homes by tomorrow morning. They will be similar in scope to the five principles introduced in today's earlier news broadcast. I know you have questions, so I have invited a single representative from all major news organizations to this little chat, and I will take questions from them now. Yes, Kate?"

"Mr....ah...what do we call you?"

"Come on, Kate. You know me. Just call me Brother Clark."

"Okay, Brother Clark. Would you really use another nuke on American soil if people don't go along with what you refer to as a social experiment?"

"Yup. Next question. Okay, Frank," Clark quipped.

"Okay, Brother Clark, who's running the country? How are taxes handled? How are the country's bills being paid?" asked Frank Cannon of CEN.

"Not to worry, Frank. I guess I'm running things until we get the Red and Blue Nations going. Of course, we have Admiral Choi and the armed forces making sure things run smoothly during this transitional period and also protecting us from foreign intervention at home and abroad. All the state and local governments should just keep on running and do what they do. The federal agencies, such as Social Security and Medicare, will also continue working as usual," explained Clark.

"Maggie, you're next," said Clark as he beckoned to the red-faced reporter in the navy suit.

"First of all, Brother *Jackass*, I don't like you! I never liked you and your ridiculous Christianized Nationalism. What gives you the right to do this to our nation?" asked Maggie Morris curtly.

"Nukes, Maggie, nukes. And by the way, I never liked you either," chuckled Clark. "Well, I better wrap this up before things get nasty. Just remember, folks, I know this is really new, but we are all going to be fine. Y'all get a good night's sleep and get ready to live out your convictions in the new nation of your choice. We'll talk again real soon. Goodnight and God bless!" said Clark with a big grin.

The looting started almost immediately following Clark's address to the nation. There was no rioting, just looting based on fear. General Choi had already deployed the military in an effort to keep order; however, as fear and panic swept the country, clashes with the military were happening all over the fifty states. In Atlanta, Los Angeles, and other large cities, the looters broke through the military lines and stormed into retail stores in an effort to steal goods that might be traded for food. The initial shots were fired in Pittsburg as hundreds of looters attacked a wholesale food warehouse. The first person to fall was a young female soldier who took a bullet to the brain. Her comrades opened up their automatic weapons on the crowd, and forty-nine civilians lay dead or dying in the streets. The company commander was horrified by his troops' response and called for a cease-fire before more carnage was realized. The soldiers retreated and attempted to restrain the crowd with batons. However, the crazed crowd broke through the lines and emptied the warehouse before reinforcements could support the outmatched troops.

The local law enforcement and first responder agencies joined the fray to protect their individual communities, but diversionary fires were set in order to draw police, fire, and military forces away from intended objectives. The news agencies were reporting by 8 a.m. the next morning that over 600 American citizens had been killed or wounded by the armed forces. Undisclosed numbers of military casualties were also reported. The local city and county jails were used as holding centers to get the people off the streets.

Brother Clark took to the airwaves again at nine the following morning to address the nation. Most people never attempted to go to work or school as fear and disbelief shook the nation to the core.

"Hello, America!" Brother Clark drawled. "I'm so sorry about last night. I guess I underestimated the fear factor involved in the changes our society is undergoing. My sincere apologies to the nation and to those who lost loved ones in last night's melee. However, I understand that Admiral Choi's forces now control every city in America, and we are secure and ready to move forward together.

"I want to introduce Seth Goldstein to you. Seth is my number one advisor and chief administrator of our Red Blue Management Team (RBMT). You know Seth as a news anchor and ace reporter. Please, Seth, come speak to America," said Clark.

Seth Goldstein was a tall and extremely handsome thirty-five-year-old who held PhDs in political science and psychology from Harvard University. Seth was a familiar face to many Americans as he had worked as a chief Washington correspondent for a major news conglomerate. Seth's likeability and engaging smile immediately put people at ease. Plus, Seth was Jewish and politically progressive, not a conservative preacher from Texas. The fact that Seth and Clark were working together was an interesting and good sign to the average viewer.

Seth flashed a huge friendly smile and began, "Hello, friends! I am so sorry for the loss of your loved ones last night. Maybe I should have appeared with Clark in the initial broadcast to let you know that I am a big part of this new system. Actually, Clark contacted me over four years ago, and we, along with a group of both conservative and progressive thinkers, put the idea of two cyber nations together. Please believe me when I say that this change will be wonderful! Imagine a country of progressive thinkers with their own prime minister and legislative body. We will be completely unfettered by conservative-based restrictions. We can set our own tax rates and live under our own laws. The conservatives can do the same. Both cyber nations will pay a central Facilitation and Administration Agency for basic infrastructure, policing, and utilities. It will be a dream world for we progressives, and the conservative citizens can be just as narrow-minded as they please in their own little world. So, don't be afraid. Go to work today and tomorrow, and then enjoy a great weekend. Send your children back to school, where the teachers will explain what is happening on an age-appropriate level. I assure you that the grocery stores and all other merchandise outlets are being restocked under the watchful eyes of Admiral Choi and her forces. So, look for emails on your NewAmerica.net computerized account that will explain the intricacies of this system and answer 99 percent of your questions."

When the holocast ended, Seth walked the few paces to Clark's desk and sighed, "This had *better* work."

"It will work, my friend. As the people realize that we are setting them free to live out their ideological dreams, they will hail us as modern creators of peace and prosperity for all."

"But what about the identification tattoos for each citizen?" asked Seth.

"They will accept the ID tattoos. We just have to make it fun," laughed Clark.

CHAPTER 2

Ready, Set, Go!

Over the next three months, the country settled back into its regular routine, as 99 percent of the citizens adjusted to not having a federal government in place. Services continued with little problem, as state and local governments operated in a normal fashion. Former federal agencies, now called National Support Agencies, operated in their normal inefficient manner but with no legislative or executive branches to make and enforce new laws and regulations. The money in the federal treasury was still in the various banks that held it before, but it had been appropriated by the RBMT to pay the bills and collect revenue.

Without a Senate and House of Representatives, no new federal laws were being created, but the laws of the states were being upheld by their own law enforcement and judicial systems. The federal judicial system no longer existed, but the inmates in federal prisons continued to be incarcerated until their sentences had been served. When they were released, they chose a nation.

Clark and Seth appeared on HV regularly to update the Red Nation and Blue Nation registration status. After the citizens had chosen their respective countries, the Blue citizens outnumbered the Red citizens 61 percent to 39 percent.

Clark, Seth, and Admiral Choi also introduced the rest of their RBMT to the country in a special two-hour holocast that was carried by all the major media outlets.

Former Secretary of State Charles Sikes was greatly revered as a dealmaker and diplomat. His legendary skills were clearly displayed in getting the other major democratic nations to join the USA in developing an anti-terrorism coalition that would fight extremism as a united force. This coalition proved invaluable when the early Middle Eastern skirmishes began that led to the Jihadist War. Secretary Sikes was a strict constitutionalist and a conservative icon. Sikes was also the son of a Baptist minister and held strong convictions about the sanctity of life. Sikes had worked for both Democrat and Republican presidents due to his skills on the international scene. Charles Sikes also took the lead as America's number one negotiator when the international community designed, tested, and employed the Nuclear Defense Alignment Treaty.

HV personality and minority rights activist Maria Cortez was well known to the public and within governmental circles. Her failed Senate run in 2026 had convinced her that external change was necessary to help the "suffering minority," and it could be better achieved through the media than through being bogged down in the Senate. Even though she hated Clark Johnson and all he stood for, she relished the idea of the Blue Nation. Maria had also hosted a popular talk show in the early 2030s that examined the national and international news from a purely progressive viewpoint.

Finally, Leon Brown, CEO of Brown Enterprises, had been an outspoken conservative voice for over a decade. An African American, Leon Brown's voice was heard on major HV networks on a regular basis, plus his podcasts had millions of subscribers. Brown's amazing "rags to riches" story had become a beacon of hope to inner-city kids and adults alike. His scholarship programs for young people had developed him a strong following among progressives as well as conservative thinkers.

After the holocast, Clark called a meeting with the entire RBMT.

Seth spoke first, "The initial feedback has been positive for our whole Transition America Initiative. Clark and I both believe that it is the proper time to reveal the new flags and identification tattoos in a single event. Then we will appoint the Red prime minister and Blue prime minister along with their lawmakers on a separate occasion. After those positions are in place, each nation will begin to mold itself based on citizen input. The excitement will be contagious!"

Clark spoke up, "Maria, are you ready to be introduced as prime minister of the Blues?"

"Yes, Clark. I am most definitely ready. I have dreamt of this day for years. I have already sent my list of ten lawmakers to each of your private accounts and await your okays," said Maria with great enthusiasm.

"How 'bout you, Charles?" Clark drawled. "Are you ready to take charge of the Red Nation?"

"Yes, sir. My lawmakers have already been approved by the entire team, and we are ready to go. I believe we are on the cusp of something great for the American people," stated Charles.

"Good. We will introduce the flags and tattoos Sunday evening and then install you both into your new offices the following Sunday."

Clark walked wearily down to his bunker in the Christian Nationalist complex. The walk down the four flights of stairs was easy and always helped him clear his mind, but he normally took the elevator back up to the operations floor as physical exercise was not something Clark was fond of. His financial contributors had no idea that they had built him not only a beautiful mansion and holovision center but also a series of underground fortified bunkers that employed over a hundred heavily armed guards and a myriad of technicians that serviced his huge, computerized ministry and now tactical systems for the RBMT. Clark even housed his personal physician and family in one of the elite bunkers. Clark Johnson was ready for anything.

Clark engaged the retinal scan at his bunker door and stepped into his lavish living quarters. As Clark strode through the marble-floored foyer, he noticed that a bulb was out in the crystal chandelier that hung over the mahogany dining table. Clark scowled about the dark light bulb as he passed through the priceless works of art that led to his private den. Julianne was sitting cross-legged on the overstuffed leather couch. Julianne was Clark's only surviving close family member. At the age of eight, Julianne lost her mother to ovarian cancer, and her older brother Tommy was killed during the final months of the Jihadist War. Julianne had just finished her daily workout in the compound gym and was sipping a glass of chilled green tea. Her long auburn hair and striking blue eyes crowned her trim figure. She greeted Clark with a cheerful, "Hi, Pops! How's the business of changing American society going today?"

Clark kissed her cheek as he chuckled, "Hey, Julianne! How is the most beautiful biologist without a real job doing today?"

They both had a hearty laugh as Clark poured himself a glass of red wine and plopped down on the rich leather sofa opposite his twenty-eight-year-old daughter.

"I wish your mother was here to see how beautiful you have become," Clark said solemnly.

"I wish she were here too, Dad. I knew so little of her. I remember her kindness, her commitment to the Lord, and her tinkling laugh. She home-schooled me until two months before she died. She was a brave and generous woman," Julianne said quietly.

"Anyone would have to be brave to live with me all those years, sweetheart! She was a jewel. Oh, anything else to report on those final test trials of the isotope-infused tattoos?" asked Clark as he purposefully changed the subject.

"The trials went perfectly, Pops. The chemical isotopic infusions will direct the DNA samples of each person to the scanner receptors in each tattoo. The application process takes about five minutes under a heat source of a hundred degrees or higher, and the skin bonding process makes the tattoos permanent. The tattoos can be affixed with a hairdryer or even by standing in the sunshine on a hot day. The tattoos and instructions are packaged and ready to be dispensed at your direction," said Julianne.

"Perfect, my dear! We will introduce them along with the new flags on Sunday night's HV broadcast. The flags and tattoos will begin to build comradery among the citizens of each country," said Clark with a huge smile.

Clark and Julianne separated with a slight hug and went into their respective luxury suites. Julianne reached her living room, and her thoughts drifted back to her mom. How would her mom feel about all this? Dividing the United States into two separate nations seemed insane, but actually, the country was already bitterly divided into progressive and conservative factions. Julianne wasn't so sure her mom would approve. Suddenly, Julianne's thoughts were broken as Seth slipped out of the shadows and embraced her. She redirected his kiss to her cheek by turning her head and burying her head into his chest as she quietly sobbed.

"We just can't do this anymore! It's wrong," Julianne whispered through her tears.

"But I love you, sweetheart, and I know you love me!" said Seth as he gazed into Julianne's blue eyes.

"Of course, I love you, Seth! But my father trusts us both to stay on course with this project. I am his daughter, and you are his closest confidant. We would break his heart! Besides, you are a Jew, and I am a Christian. I am Red, and you are Blue. We must put our feelings aside for the good of the nations."

Seth lifted Julianne's head up tenderly and caressed her lips softly. She responded by kissing him with all her passion while tears streamed down her cheeks. They held each other in a warm embrace for a few minutes before Seth silently exited the side door.

Clark had monitored the whole thing on the handheld device he called "Snoopy." He slowly shook his head and sighed deeply. Clark knew the affair was going on but was giving Julianne time to break it off before he confronted them both.

Clark poured himself another glass of red wine and let his thoughts drift back to his childhood. Clark remembered the humiliation of being the smallest and poorest kid in his fourth-grade class in Tupelo, Mississippi. He could still feel the emotional pain of rejection as he remembered the catcalls from the group of athletic boys that mocked his attempts to hit a baseball or kick a soccer ball. Because Clark's home was near the school, he walked the half-mile distance every morning and afternoon. Clark's mom was always working, and his dad was not around, so he was never driven to school by his parents. His mom never attended a PTA meeting or a school play. She just worked. No one was there to help Clark when Mrs. Green's mean dog barked viciously at him as he walked down 23rd Street. Sometimes the dog would actually chase Clark while nipping at his heels. Clark was so afraid of the dog that he sometimes took the longer route home via 25th Street. But that didn't help at all because an older boy on that street would laugh at Clark and shoot him with a BB gun. He could almost feel the sting of the BBs as they hit against the tee-shirt that covered his boney back. Clark lived a life of fear and dread outside of the classroom.

Inside the educational facility, however, Clark was extremely gifted. He was the smartest kid in his class, and all the teachers loved him. He was a whizz at maths and science and made his only Bs in PE. Clark had been given a full scholarship in electrical engineering to Mississippi State University but turned it down and went to seminary instead. Clark felt like he was called by God to help Americans believe in their country, as well as Jesus. Clark passionately believed that America had been founded on biblical principles, but the Washington politicians didn't believe in the Bible and were not cooperating with God's plan for the country. Clark tried to work within the political system for years, but the country was totally deadlocked between liberals and conservatives. Actually, it was that political and social gridlock that spawned the idea of two cyber nations. Clark Johnson saw himself as American society's savior.

CHAPTER 3

Where Is Captain America?

The tattoos had been delivered to each individual family with instructions for application. This phase of the plan had gone well, except for some conservative Christians who thought the tattoos might be the "Mark of the Beast" as described in the biblical book of Revelation. To complicate matters, it was decreed by Clark that double arm amputees should affix the tattoo to their forehead. Clark had managed to somewhat soothe the Christian Right by quoting a myriad of Bible verses regarding biblical prophecy in a lengthy HV address, but still, there was lingering doubt and mistrust toward the tattoos.

In a grand ceremony that was broadcast worldwide, Prime Minister Maria Cortez was installed as the leader of the Blue Nation, and Prime Minister Charles Sikes was installed as head of the Reds. Each of their ten lawmakers was also installed in a grand display of unity and cooperation. Clark explained that each nation would become operational on January 15th. The remaining weeks would be spent making sure all wireless programming was completed for each respective Red or Blue household. It was explained with much fanfare that although the lawmakers would suggest laws in keeping with the cultural and political leanings of each nation, it would take an actual 51 percent vote by the citizens to enact any law. The Red and Blue Nations were not republics as the USA had been; they were actual democracies. There was no president, no Congress, no Senate, and no Electoral College. The states still existed but were no longer united as they had been under the U. S. federal government. The governors and other state officials now enjoyed more power without a federal government to deal with. The Red and Blue Nations would exist in all fifty states but would recognize "states' rights" to a much greater degree than under the former U. S. federal government. The grand experiment would begin shortly.

The Christmas season was filled with great anticipation in the month before the nations went "live." Many Christmas trees were decorated according to the Red or Blue nations' colors. There was even a blue costumed Santa Claus sitting right next to the red one in most malls. Christmas cards that always favored red and green now appeared in blue and green hues as well.

Christmas toys took on a blue or red nationalist flavor. There was even a totally blue Spiderman and a completely red Superman marketed with other superhero figures, but Captain America was nowhere to be found.

The flags of the two nations were a popular Christmas gift. The Blue Nation's flag was embossed with a white dove in flight with the words "Peace, Equality, and Justice" emblazoned across the top. The background was a beautiful medium blue. The Red Nation's flag was a deep red similar to the original color of the old American flag, and it had the head of a bald eagle in the center with the slogan "Peace and Prosperity Through Strength" in bold gold-colored letters under the eagle's head. Flags were displayed on houses, buildings, book-bags, T-shirts, and vehicle bumpers. The nations were each finding their unique identity.

January 15 was declared to be Dual Nations Day and a joint holiday for years to come. Schools and businesses closed, and people spent much of the day at their Ameriputer as the prime ministers and lawmakers sent out basic law suggestions that were voted on by the two nations. Many families barbecued out in the South or played snow games in the North as the whole populaces displayed their colors. Many homeowners painted their front doors either blue or red, while renters covered their doors in red or blue foil. It was truly a magical time as the two countries began to function in glorious autonomy.

* * * * *

Seth and Julianne faced each other as they stood before the county magistrate. Julianne thought she could feel the new life moving inside her as she said her wedding vows to Seth. A baby. She was going next week to confirm the gender of their child. The magistrate's words jolted her back to the present.

"Julianne, repeat after me. With this ring…"

Julianne was again broken away from her thoughts as she heard the words, "I now pronounce you Seth and Julianne Johnson-Goldstein."

What a disappointment. Julianne had always wanted a big church wedding with her father as the officiant. What a fool she was. No white dress. No bridesmaids. No wedding presents. Just a five-minute ceremony with a government official she had never met before. She loved Seth dearly, but getting pregnant was totally stupid! Why didn't they use birth control? Seth had lobbied for an abortion, but Julianne's pro-life stance was unyielding. They would have this baby, love it, and raise it together. But how would they tell Clark? He was not going to be happy!

Seth kissed Julianne quickly, and the wedding was over. Julianne wiped away a tear as they left the magistrate's office.

*****

The Red Constitution was ratified by 78 percent of the Red voters only five weeks later. The Red Constitution mirrored the U. S. Constitution in many ways but added provisions that allowed swifter prosecution, fast-track sentencing, and harsher penalties for murder, rape, and drug trafficking. In fact, the penalty for illegal drug production and distribution was death by hanging in the town square.

The first public hanging was carried out in the small town of Saxton, Missouri. The chief perpetrator, William Cole, was a known "pixie dust" manufacturer and distributor. Cole established his drug labs in small communities and then shipped his product to the major cities and local dealers. He and the seven people who ran his local drug lab were hung together on a Saturday morning. Clark Johnson, along with the Red prime minister, attended the event along with a huge security detail. The gallows had been constructed only a week before. The eight criminals—six men and two women— were marched into the tiny town square adjacent to the courthouse, where a crowd of Red citizens booed and hissed as the offenders begged for mercy. The crowd had been sufficiently fired up by testimonials from people who had lost family members to pixie dust overdoses.

The crowd was shouting "hang 'em!—hang 'em!—hang 'em!" when the trap doors dropped.

The eight criminals struggled and made animal-like sounds as the life drained out of them. The fortunate ones sustained a broken neck immediately and died almost instantly. Others thrashed about at the end of the rope while feces and urine stained their orange jumpsuits. It took the last one, a slender woman of twenty-four, almost two full minutes to stop moving. The crowd was totally silent while the bodies were taken down and ceremoniously pronounced dead by the local coroner. It took a few minutes for the coroner to do his job, as faint heartbeats can still be detected in hanging victims for several minutes after their ordeal.

PM Charles Sikes stood with Clark at his side to speak to the shocked crowd, "My fellow citizens, we have all witnessed a horrific sight today. We have witnessed the horrible and violent death of eight criminals that have preyed on our young people by peddling poison. While what we have seen is unsettling, it is also a just punishment for these merchants of death. May all criminals in both nations be warned that justice is swift and sure in the Red Nation."

The news services covered the hangings with great enthusiasm. The videos of the eight criminals dying by hanging were the top lead story on every news service for the next few days. Since news services were all owned by corporations, the tone of the stories agreed with the philosophies of the nation to which the news organization corporations belonged.

Blue citizens organized protest marches in Birmingham, Alabama, and San Francisco, California, but they were largely ignored. Clark noted on his weekly holocast that to protest what was going on in the Red Nation was not only foolish but none of the Blue citizens' business.

"You Blue folks don't protest what's going on in Saudi Arabia, so why would you protest what your sister nation does? If you don't want to hang drug manufacturers and traffickers in the Blue Nation, then don't hang 'em!" Clark smirked.

The Blue Nation Constitution was ratified about six weeks later. The Blue Constitution contained no capital punishment provisions but did include mandatory government-sponsored rehabilitation services for drug traffickers and violent offenders.

*****

Seth and Julianne had made an appointment with Clark for a Tuesday morning and waited nervously for him to invite them into his plush office. After they were seated in front of his huge, cluttered desk, Julianne spoke first.

"Dad, there is something Seth and I need to tell you," Julianne said softly.

"Do you think I don't know about your pathetic relationship and your sham marriage?" Clark asked sarcastically. "Marriages can be annulled, you know."

Julianne was shaken but refused to cry or back down. "Dad, Seth and I love each other. And there is more. I am carrying his baby and your grandchild. You are going to have a grandson. We want to name him Clark Johnson Goldstein and call him Little Clark."

Clark was dumbfounded. He knew about the marriage but not about the baby. As Clark regained his composure, he slowly rose and gave Julianne a tight hug and then offered his hand to Seth. "Welcome to the family, Seth. I'm not happy about your taking advantage of my daughter, but I fully accept you as my son-in-law," said a now somber Clark.

Seth knew to say absolutely nothing as he clumsily grasped and quickly shook his new father-in-law's hand.

CHAPTER 4

The Breach

Admiral Choi finished her 6.2-mile morning run and got a quick shower. After dressing in full uniform, she wolfed down her plain bagel topped with cream cheese and grabbed a cup of black coffee on her way out the door. Most generals and admirals lived in luxurious housing, but Choi lived in a two-bedroom apartment only fifteen minutes from the Pentagon. Her apartment had a full gym with mirrored walls in one bedroom, while the other bedroom was reserved for Choi and her two beagles, Brutus and Pancake.

Choi's military guard detail pulled out into traffic ahead of her two-year-old Audi RT Sport 400 and switched on the blue lights and siren that launched the secure trip to her Pentagon office. As she stepped out of the vehicle, the guard detail saluted as she entered the front of the building. Choi loved grand entrances, whether it was as mundane as going to work or as exciting as a surprise attack with her SEAL Group. At forty-eight years of age, Choi was still full of energy and authority. Her coal-black eyes were deeply set in her pleasant but makeup-free Asian American face. Choi was a tall, lean woman and extremely muscular. She was not one to be toyed with.

Admiral Choi, or Nancy to her childhood friends, was a science/math geek, an athlete, and pretty enough to be in beauty pageants which she never bothered to enter. Why should she waste her time looking for physical approval when she was busy winning science fairs and playing power forward on her high school basketball team. There were boys, but seldom did her relationships last more than a few dates. Nancy became bored easily and moved on to her next conquest. She wasn't against love and romance but never seemed to have time to pursue a serious commitment. You don't become a SEAL team leader and an admiral by wasting precious time.

Choi entered the joint chiefs' conference room and greeted her fellow commanders. The other six joint chiefs plus their various aides were already assembling. Also, the directors of the CIA and National Bureau of Investigation (former FBI) were in attendance. Choi's chief aide spoke a few words into her handheld device, and a holographic image of Choi's agenda appeared at each station. After the first few mundane items, Choi said, "Okay, Mr. NBI Director, tell us about the hack attempts."

Johnathan Weeks had been the FBI director under two presidents and now fulfilled the NBI director's office for the Red and Blue Nations. Weeks had dedicated thirty-five years to service in the FBI and was seen as competent and dedicated.

"Admiral Choi, the hack attempts are coming from somewhere in this mainland but have not penetrated the firewalls to a substantial degree at this time. The CIA assures me that the attacks are not foreign-based. The most interesting feature of the attacks is that they are all targeting the Red Nation servers," said Johnathan Weeks.

"Does that lead us to believe that a Blue citizen organization is behind these attacks?" queried Admiral Choi.

"Yes, ma'am. With the Blue Nation's higher tax rates and lower number of working citizens, the Blue Nation is already struggling to pay its federal infrastructure bills. We think they are trying to pirate money from the Red coffers."

"But they haven't succeeded yet?"

"No, ma'am...not yet."

*****

Clark Johnson sipped his glass of 2017 Jean-Louis Chavy burgundy and thought about the news of his grandson. A grandson! His firstborn, Tommy, had lost his life in the Jihadist War, and Clark had been devastated. His son was everything Clark was not: tall, muscular, naturally athletic, and masculine. Even though Clark loved Julianne dearly, Tommy had always been his favorite. He had been killed by the grenade of an enemy fighter as his squad of Marines was clearing out underground communication tunnels in Syria. Tommy's body was shipped home in a flag-draped coffin. Clark had wept for weeks. And now another male Johnson was on the horizon.

"Thank You, Lord, for this grandson," Clark whispered as he wiped away a few tears.

Maybe this marriage would work. Seth was a good man, and Julianne seemed to really love him. There were plenty of other Red-Blue couples that had good marriages. Yes, this would work. Clark would help make it work.

Clark finished his third glass of wine, wiped his eyes, and made his way down the long hall to his four-poster bed. A good night's rest would soothe the turbulent emotions engulfing this new world leader and soon-to-be grandfather.

While most of the Red Nation's administrative team slept, a black-clad figure entered the five-digit lock code at supply door number four of the Red Nation's remote server location and slipped inside.

A guard called out, "Halt, or you're dead."

"It's me, Henry. I'm just a little late," said the dark figure in a quiet female voice.

"Password?" demanded the guard.

"Delta Switch," said the woman.

"Okay, follow me," the burly guard responded.

Henry Wilson escorted the woman into the main server room and quietly demanded, "Okay, where's my fifty grand?"

"You didn't think I was going to bring it in paper money, did you?" the sinister figure chuckled. "It's in your offshore account as we agreed."

"Okay," Henry muttered as he walked cautiously back to his post.

Henry was in financial trouble and saw this act of treason as a necessary evil to take care of his family and help his daughter through her final year of college. Henry's wife of twenty-six years was confined to a wheelchair due to a spinal injury caused when Henry ran a stop sign. He never forgave himself and had spent most of his money taking his wife to specialists instead of the government-approved doctors supplied by the Blue Nation. His dear Ethel only grew worse, and Henry suffered in a world of self-doubt, guilt, and shame.

The dark figure surveyed the numerous servers until she spotted #017. She opened the face of the server and simply added a small microchip board to the open slot just to the right of the motherboard network. She smiled, closed up the server, and crept back toward the guard desk. Henry seemed nervous as the slim figure approached. Henry was about to say, "Be quiet leaving..." when he felt the needle in his neck. Without remorse, she dragged Henry to door number four and keyed it open. Her accomplices were waiting. They secured the door, zipped Henry into a body bag, and carried the unconscious guard beyond the open gate to the supply area where a black van was waiting for them. Henry Wilson was never seen or heard from again.

Clark Johnson was alerted by his chief security guard at 6 a.m. the next morning. There was a serious problem, and the RBMT was being assembled in the main conference room of the compound.

Admiral Choi spoke first, "Sir, there has been a serious monetary breach in the system."

"What in God's name do you mean, Nancy? I thought the hacking attempts were little more than annoyances," asked an exasperated Clark.

"The system wasn't hacked, Clark. It was manually disrupted, and 10 trillion dollars were removed from the Red Nation system and deposited into the Blue Nation operating account, where it has been moved offshore and used to pay Blue Nation debt. The money is gone!"

"What can we do?" said Clark as he shook his head slowly from side to side.

"We can't transfer it back at present as the account is encrypted. We don't even know who planned the attack. We only know why," said Nancy.

"Right, the Blue Nation has been whining for months about having too many deadbeats among their citizens," offered Clark.

"Now wait a minute, Clark!" screeched Maria Cortez, the Blue prime minister.

"Don't yell at me, Maria! You Blues ratified your own constitution, set your own tax rates, and are self-governing. Have you forgotten that little fact?" Clark said with an incredulous look.

"Exactly," chimed in Charles Sikes, the Red prime minister. "It's not our fault your country is broke, but it is your responsibility to return the money your country stole from mine!"

"Everybody shut up!" Seth boomed at the top of his voice. "We are in this together. Accusing each other and screaming will not bring stability and get the money returned to the proper owner."

The RBMT issued a news release at about 10 a.m., and both nations knew about the theft shortly before noon. The news release included an appeal by Clark and Seth for patience as the problem was resolved and offered a reward for information concerning this robbery of the Red Nation coffers.

The first act of violence occurred in Tampa, Florida, when a Red Nation citizen went next door and demanded payment from his Blue neighbor. Dr. Robert Daniels, PhD, had just come in from the local community college where he worked as a sociology professor. After hearing loud pounding on his blue front door, Robert opened the door to see his neighbor Clyde Matthews with clenched fists and a bright red face.

"Hey, Clyde. What's wrong?" asked Robert.

"I'll take my $55,000," hissed Clyde.

"What are you talking about, neighbor?" queried Robert.

"That's what you Blue idiots owe every man, woman, and child in the Red Nation!"

"Now, wait a minute, Clyde—"

Robert never saw the fourteen-inch pipe wrench Clyde had hidden behind his back before it crashed into the left side of his head, breaking his jaw and fracturing his skull. Robert tumbled back into his foyer and struck his head on the tile surface with a dull thud. Clyde dragged Robert along the sidewalk, leaving a trail of bright red blood. Clyde rolled Robert onto the curb location normally reserved for household garbage containers and then walked toward his red door muttering, "Sorry liberal Blue trash! Always trying to take money from working folks to spend on their social programs…"

Reports of Red citizens attacking their Blue work colleagues and neighbors began to be reported in most areas of the country. The local police treated most altercations like domestic disputes until a group of armed Red citizens took over a restaurant in Kentucky and began to force the Blue patrons to empty their bank accounts via electronic devices. Of course, the funds were funneled into the bank accounts of the Red citizens holding them at gunpoint.

Once again, the two countries were put under martial law for a time until all could be sorted out. Since 75 percent of law enforcement and military personnel were Red citizens, many of the Red Nation aggressors were dispersed but not arrested. There were three other deaths in Tampa, along with Robert Daniels.

Not all of the conflict between the citizens of the two nations was violent. At a neighborhood homeowners association gathering in Indiana, the mood became so ugly that all of the Red citizens were voted off the HOA board and dismissed from the meeting.

Not all confrontations began as unpleasant. A Red citizen in Mobile, Alabama, was standing in line behind a Blue citizen at the grocery store when the Blue citizen's credit card was declined. The Red citizen quietly offered to pay for the Blue citizen's groceries, but the Blue citizen became enraged and screamed, "I would rather starve than take the filthy money from a Red Nation fool that hangs people for minor offenses!" The customers around the cash register began to take sides, and a shouting match ensued that could have led to violence if not for a quick call to 911 that swiftly produced a police squad car that was patrolling on a nearby street.

After an uneasy peace had been restored across the land, Clark, with the whole team standing at his side, addressed the nation. "My friends," Clark began, "even though we are two separate nations now, our Red and Blue citizens have a unique bond. We are still one people living on one soil. We work together, go to church together, and share families together. I assure you that no one on our team perpetrated this financial attack, and we have found a way to temporarily restore the Red Nation funds until the real thieves can be caught and brought to justice. Maria, would you please share the details?"

The camera shifted to Maria Cortez, the Blue prime minister, and she began to speak.

"First, I would like to assure the Red Nation that your Blue neighbors and our Blue government had nothing to do with the loss of your resources. We are appalled that this theft took place and have proposed a solution that your Red PM and government have accepted on your behalf."

Charles Sikes, the Red prime minister, moved next to Maria and nodded approval as she continued.

"We have borrowed 10 trillion dollars from the World Bank and secured it with several National Parks that are jointly owned by our two great nations. We have also relinquished our part of the joint ownership of additional parks and recreation areas that will equal the $10 trillion owed."

Charles Sikes spoke, "My fellow Red countrymen, we appreciate the willingness of the Blue Nation's leadership to solve this problem temporarily. I assure you that we will find the true thieves. Until then, live at peace with your Blue neighbors. God bless you, and good night!"

As the cameras ceased filming, Maria glared at Charles, "I can't believe you forced me into this ridiculous deal! We not only gave up our share of the National Parks as collateral for the World Bank, but we also gave you our part of several major jointly owned national properties. You, sir, are a greedy extortionist!"

Charles chuckled, "Aw, c'mon, Maria, all you have to do is levy another tax on your poor Blue citizens. Besides, it's better than hanging from one of our Red gallows after you were convicted of espionage and grand theft."

Maria walked away briskly while cursing in Spanish.

CHAPTER 5

Watson Strikes Back

"That was perfect! Perfect!" roared former President Kennedy Watson. "They never expected an old-fashioned hardware attack on their server. They were expecting a cyber assault. Well done! Well done!"

Kennedy Watson was not one to go quietly into the night. Watson was going to get *his* country back. The assembled group of former Senators, House members, and marginalized military leaders smiled, laughed, and nodded in agreement.

"So, what's the next step, boss?" George Turner, Watson's former chief of staff, asked.

"The next step is to stay invisible, George. Preacher Clark and his band of revolutionaries can keep busy running their little social experiment while we continue to sow discord in their utopias. As much as I hate Clark Johnson, I'm almost glad he pulled this coup," said Watson.

"I don't understand, Mr. President. What good can come out of Johnson's betrayal of America?"

"Think about it, George. We've been trying to get rid of the Electoral College in favor of 'one man, one vote' since the Trump years, and that idiot preacher did it for us! Now, all we have to do is put the country back together, and the progressive agenda will be the norm for the foreseeable future—or as Brother Clark would say, 'Until Jesus comes.'"

The whole room burst into laughter and applause.

"Plus, I have another little surprise coming for Clark…"

*****

Julianne finished her charity run and was preparing to shower and change before she addressed the crowd at the Denver YMCA. Even at six and a half months pregnant, Julianne looked great. She was absolutely stunning with her auburn hair, fair skin, and bright blue eyes. She had finished the 5K run in 23:54 minutes, which wouldn't have been a bad time if she weren't pregnant. The male security guards assigned to Julianne were outside the single entrance to the women's locker room. Inside the locker room, Julianne chatted with Meriam, her aide and female security guard, and the cleaning lady that had been busy making sure the changing area was spotless. Carol Bond, the cleaning lady, was a tall, slender woman of about forty-five with bottle-blonde hair and a quick smile. Carol talked about her children and two-year-old grandson as she tirelessly wiped down the counters and inspected the area for anything out of place.

"Here, let me show you a picture of my little man," chuckled Carol.

As Julianne and Meriam moved closer to view the grandbaby on Carol's phone, Carol cleanly felled Meriam with a single roundhouse kick to the head. Julianne froze in her tracks and clutched her midsection.

Carol whispered, "Okay, missy, if you make a sound, I will deliver the same kick to that big belly of yours. Now be still while I put this 'sleep' patch on you."

Carol applied the patch, and Julianne sunk into a deep drug-induced sleep. Carol caught her and gently stuffed her into her large rolling garbage can and then covered the sleeping woman with plastic bags and cleaning tools. She then rolled the sleeping Julianne right past the agents guarding the door to the locker room entrance. Carol pushed Julianne to the boiler room, where she was met by a woman dressed in a food service uniform; both women removed Julianne from the garbage can and placed her inside an empty food service cart. Carol removed her blonde wig revealing a short brown hairstyle, and after quickly changing into a food service uniform, Carol and her accomplice rolled Julianne out to a white van in the parking lot. They put the cart containing Julianne into the back of the van and cinched it down with bungee cords so it wouldn't roll. Then they simply drove away.

Julianne awoke a few hours later with a huge headache and mild nausea. She was lying on a small bed in a damp gray concrete room with an old-style bare bulb fluorescent light fixture as the only source of illumination. There was a stainless-steel toilet on one side of the room with a stainless-steel sink a couple of feet away. A half roll of toilet paper and a paper cup rested on a metal shelf above the toilet. The smell of mold and cigarette smoke drifted through the dank little dungeon. Julianne began to shiver as she was still wearing only her sleeveless running outfit.

Julianne tried the massive gray door that appeared to be the only exit but found it securely locked. A sudden feeling of dread dropped on Julianne as she made her way to the stainless-steel toilet. When Julianne finished up her use of the smelly toilet, she was horrified to see fresh, bright red blood on the tissue.

"Oh my God! I'm spotting!" sobbed Julianne.

Julianne dropped to her knees on the cold concrete floor and sobbed as great waves of sadness swept over her. "Dear Lord," she mouthed between sobs, "please help my baby and me! He is not ready to be born yet, and I have no idea where I am or how to help him! Oh, God, please, please help us..."

"So, is our conservative princess upset? Maybe that good-looking husband of yours will appear at any moment to whisk you away to safety, little darling!" Carol taunted.

Julianne looked up through her tears to see Carol looming over her.

"Please, Carol! Do whatever you want to with me, but don't let my baby die! Please, Carol, *please!*" Julianne shouted through her tears.

Carol didn't say another word but chuckled loudly as she slammed the huge metal door behind her.

When Julianne didn't show up in time to speak after the race, her security guards entered the women's locker room and found Meriam unconscious on the floor. Meriam remembered the friendly blonde cleaning woman but little else. The security detail called the CBI (Colorado Bureau of Investigation) and began to question the YMCA staff. As suspected, there was no tall blonde cleaning woman. There was, however, a blonde wig that had been tossed into the boiler room trash along with a janitorial uniform. The empty garbage can that was used to conceal the drugged Julianne was also found in the parking lot. The CBI arrived and sent the wig and clothes to the lab for immediate DNA testing. It didn't take long to confirm that "Carol" was actually a mercenary assassin named Angelica Jacquez or *Angel Jack*, as she was known in the underworld. Angel Jack was a master of disguise, ruthless, and without conscience. She was linked to over thirty international kills and had managed to elude capture in several countries.

Clark and Seth were in the middle of a strategy meeting with their top advisors when they got the message about Julianne's kidnapping. Clark was stunned, and Seth was incredulous.

"Kidnapped! How could that possibly happen?" roared Seth.

"Julianne and Little Clark...Oh, God..." Clark moaned.

Another aide rushed in breathlessly, "He's calling! The kidnapper is calling!"

Seth snapped "Holo on," and the holovision came to life, displaying a smiling 3D image of Kennedy Watson.

"Hello, boys!" Watson said sarcastically.

"Oh, God, no!" squeaked Clark.

"You snake!" snarled Seth.

"It's good to see you too, gentlemen," Watson chuckled.

"What have you done with my wife?" thundered Seth.

"Oh, she's in a safe place, Seth. Of course, it doesn't contain the finery she is used to, but she is alive and well..."

"What about Little Clark?"

"Well, that is somewhat of a problem. Julianne is spotting...you know, bleeding a little...but that can happen in pregnancy, right?"

Clark began to sob while Seth spoke in a quiet but menacing voice, "If anything happens to either one of them, I *will* kill you, Kennedy Watson."

"Aw, come on, Seth. I wouldn't hurt your little family. And just to show good faith, here is a proof of life video."

A video of Julianne crying and looking miserable briefly flashed up and was gone.

"I assure you, Clark and Seth, my friend Angel Jack is taking excellent care of Julianne and her unborn son."

CHAPTER 6

Commandoes

As soon as Admiral Choi heard the mention of the name Angel Jack, she excused herself and slipped quietly from the room. Kennedy Watson's call had produced so much turmoil that Nancy wasn't missed. She found an empty office and immediately called her friend, former FBI special agent Sonya Arthur.

"Hey, Sonya, I—"

"Well, hey, Nan! I have missed our chats since you set out to change the country—"

"Sonya, listen to me!" Nancy barked.

"Sorry, Nan.... What's up?"

"It's Angel Jack, Sonya. She's kidnapped Julianne, and I'm sure she is holding her at the old CIA compound outside of Athens, Texas."

"That rat! I can't believe you two came from the same family! She is poison!"

"Yes, she is, and she is working with Kennedy Watson, the biggest rat of all. Can you meet me in Athens,

Texas, in a few hours, and we'll decide how to play this?" asked Admiral Choi.

"Actually, I just got out of the shower and can dress and be on my way immediately. Hey, can I bring Kirk Waters with me? He hates Angel Jack. She assassinated a foreign diplomat that Kirk was assigned to protect, and Kirk has never lived it down."

"Sure, bring him. He's good with his hands, as I recall. And Sonya...this is going to be nasty. Be ready."

Lee Choi, Nancy's father, had married a woman named Della Brown during his senior year as a cadet at West Point. Della was an RN at the local hospital close to the university. Lee and Della met at a bar that was frequented by cadets and hospital personnel and immediately began to date. After a torrid romance, Lee and Della were married just before his first deployment. Della gave birth to Nancy two years into the marriage but surprisingly left Lee and Nancy only a year later. Della quickly divorced Lee, citing his frequent trips away from home, and moved to Canada. Lee claimed that Della was fully aware that his job as part of an Army Rangers special ops unit would require his being away from home a good deal, but now Della was gone, and Lee would be responsible for raising the infant Nancy. After the nasty divorce, Nancy strongly bonded with her father and the military way of life. Little Nancy was determined to be a good soldier, just like her dad. Of course, Nancy's full scholarship to the Naval Academy resulted in her eventually becoming a SEAL rather than an Army Ranger.

Della reappeared ten years later in New York. She had married a French-Canadian named Jock Jacquez and had given birth to Angelica. The half-sisters, who were three years apart, had spent little time together but enough to dislike each other greatly. But they would be meeting again soon.

As Sonya and Kirk streaked from D. C. to Texas in their NBI jet-copter, Sonya was filled with emotions. It seemed like Nancy had always been hurt by her family. It was easy for Sonya to see Nancy's integrity and quality compared to the mother who abandoned her but raised her half-sister Angelica the assassin. Sonya blushed as she remembered her first meeting with Nancy Choi. As a tentative midshipman at the Naval Academy, Sonya had made a brief bathroom stop before her first class. She so wanted to make a good impression, but as she was about to exit the restroom, a soft touch made her pause, and a quiet voice said, "Hey, plebe, you better check that surrender flag on the bottom of your shoe! Toilet tissue will not make a good first impression on the guys who are hoping to wash you out." Sonya was grateful and intuitively knew she had met a lifelong friend and mentor in Nan.

The reduced speed of the jet-copter and Kirk's comment after leaning forward and peering out the window brought Sonya into the present. "So that's what Texas looks like," said Kirk.

*****

Julianne's bleeding had continued but at a slower rate. She tried to remain calm and pray, but the words didn't seem to come. Mental traffic invaded her mind, and she imagined a scene at a joint funeral where Seth and Clark were sobbing over two caskets—one large and one small. She trembled with fear.

"Here, princess. I brought you some food and water. Oh, and by the way, my name's not Carol; it's Angel Jack. How bout I call you Princess Julianne, and you call me Queen AJ," snickered Angel Jack.

When her captor was gone, Julianne looked in the cardboard box Angel Jack had left and found a bottle of water, an apple, and a dried-out turkey sandwich that looked like it had been sitting around quite a while as the mayonnaise had turned yellow. Julianne left the sandwich in the bag and bit into the apple.

"Oh my, this is sweet. Thank You, Lord," Julianne whispered. As Julianne finished up the apple and sipped on the water, she mused, "Angel Jack...now where have I heard that name before? Angel Jack...*Angel Jack*! Oh my God, she's the assassin!"

The sound of prayers mixed with sobs gushed out of the young wife and mother-to-be as she cried out to God for herself and the unborn Little Clark. Julianne prayed and cried for what seemed like an hour while the blood continued to slowly ooze from her womb.

*****

Sonya and Kirk met Nancy at the little diner off Highway 138 outside Athens, Texas, at about 3 p.m. that afternoon. Nancy surveyed Kirk as he walked in the front door along with Sonya. Kirk was only about five feet ten inches but solidly put together at forty-five years of age. He carried a thin scar below his right ear that was the result of his encounter with Angel Jack's stiletto. The larger scar where she knifed him under the rib cage was only visible with his shirt off. Kirk had barely survived the attack and was anxious for some old-fashioned revenge.

They ate a late lunch and planned their rescue of Julianne and their conquest of Angel Jack.

"So, Nan," began Sonya, "why are you so sure Angel Jack is holding Julianne in this area?"

"I know exactly where she is. When Kennedy played the proof of life video, we could all see that she was in a prison-like atmosphere. But I noticed two small portals in the wall above the stainless-steel toilet in the background. Those portals only exist at CIA black sites."

"What's the purpose of the portals?" asked Kirk.

"One of the portals is a tiny speaker through which subliminal information is relayed to the prisoner. It merely sounds like a mechanical hissing noise, but the messages plant the idea of cooperation into the prisoner's mind. The second portal emits an odorless gaseous form of sodium amytal that is akin to the old truth serums but airborne. Even prisoners that don't respond to other forms of interrogation have to use the toilet," explained Admiral Choi.

"Wow!" exclaimed Kirk. "Never heard of this stuff."

"As you know, black sites were outlawed after the Jihadist War. There was only one on American soil—about twenty miles outside Athens, Texas. We are about twelve miles from it now. It appears to be a defunct facility, but with the generators and security systems, it is perfect for Watson's and Angel Jack's purposes. Let's check into that little roadside motel and get some rest before tonight. We leave for the compound at 0200 hours," said Nancy.

*****

Seth received a coded call on a secure line at about 6 p.m. It was Admiral Choi.

"I know where she is, Seth. I've put a team together, and we will bring her back to you. How is Clark holding up?"

"Aw, he is a basket case—you know, totally distraught. You would think a 'mighty man of God' could show a little more faith. But I can't really criticize him; I just want to get my hands around Kennedy Watson's neck and squeeze the life out of him."

"Tell Clark that I am on it. We will bring Julianne and the baby home to you both."

Clark came into Seth's office a few minutes later, and Seth told him about the rescue attempt. Clark responded with a quick smile through his tears but then told Seth about Watson's demands.

"Seth, I've got to tell the nations the truth about the nukes. Watson has sniffed it out, and I've admitted the details to him," stated Clark.

"Clark, you can't do that! The people will never forgive you. The world will never forgive you! Watson's a snake! He won't let Julianne and the baby live anyway," warned Seth.

"I'm sorry, Seth. I've got to do this. I'm just a lying preacher, and Julianne and the baby are paying for my sins. I go live on AmeriNet at 8 p.m.," said Clark before turning and swiftly walking away.

At promptly 8 p.m., Clark Johnson appeared to address the two nations. His puffy eyes and red face were evidence of his deep sorrow.

"As you already know from the news reports, my daughter and Seth's wife, Julianne, and their unborn

60

son were recently kidnapped after her charity run. I have received many messages from you—that you are praying for us and keeping us in your thoughts. We are humbled and sincerely appreciate your support at this desperate time."

Clark cleared his throat and continued, "I must tell you that I have not been totally honest with you...actually, I misled you in a terrible way, and I am ashamed of myself...but I want to make it right tonight. You see... there was never more than one nuclear bomb. I stated that we had other nuclear devices in three more American cities, but a nuclear device does not have to be a bomb. There are many medical devices in the nuclear medical field that help save people, not kill them. I lied. I more than lied—I used your fear of nuclear destruction to deceive you."

Clark took a sip of water and continued, "I am so ashamed of the lies that I used to manipulate you into forming the Red and Blue Nations. I have asked the Lord to forgive me, and now I am asking you to forgive me. I know this truth will have great ramifications for citizens of both nations, and we will work through it together, but I wanted you to know the truth. I am so deeply sorry.... Uh...good night."

At 2 a.m. that night, Nancy, Sonya, and Kirk parked about 400 yards from the facility. They each carried a backpack containing weapons and electronic equipment. They moved silently through the starless night until they reached a spot just behind the tree line, about seventy-five yards from the old black site facility. They unloaded their backpacks, revealing automatic weapons, auto-injectors, wireless tasers, and the Micro Surveillance System (MSS). Nancy entered the access code, and fifty micro-drones with infrared reading capacity whirred off into the night toward the compound.

"Put on your MSS goggles. It won't take long for the first drone readings to begin the mapping process," whispered Nancy.

The micro-drones worked in sequenced unity to map the building dimensions, interior structures, and heat signatures for people and equipment within the structure. The first readings reached the Micro Surveillance control board within a few minutes. From the control board, the system transmitted the data to the MSS goggles, where a green-lined image of the building was projected onto the goggle lenses. The projection included hot spot outlines representing computers, the heating system, and people. There were five hot spots that appeared to be five people in single beds in a large open room. There was a single hot spot in a separate room. These six appeared to be sleeping. There were four additional people stationed outside the facility in guard-like positions. There was one additional location containing what appeared to be two people. One was in the prone position, while another was standing just outside the door to the room.

"Okay, we know who they are and where they are," whispered Nan.

"We do?" mumbled Kirk.

"Sure, we do. We have four active guards, five guards sleeping, and one guard outside Julianne's location. The lone person is probably Angel Jack," whispered Sonya.

"Okay, let's move out and take care of the outside guards first, then rendezvous at the kitchen entrance. Kirk, take the guard at the north side. Sonya, get the guy on the SW corner. I will get the two at the kitchen and loading dock. No gunfire. Use the auto-injectors or tasers to render them totally silent and useless to Angel Jack. Remember, silence is your friend," said Admiral Choi quietly.

The three rescuers in their black garb moved silently through the tree line until they separated to carry out their individual missions. Sonya reached the SW corner and waited to strike until the camouflaged older man was relieving himself at the hedges close to the corner of the building. The dart from the wireless taser struck the guard in the left temple, and he collapsed on the ground into a quivering, softly groaning figure.

"Hey, didn't your mama teach you not to pee in public?" whispered Sonya with a grin as she injected a sedative into the shaking figure.

Kirk approached his guard from the rear and applied an armbar choke hold that rendered the large female unconscious in a few seconds. He quickly injected her neck with a sedative that would keep her down for hours.

Nancy moved slowly along the back of the building and hid behind the main garbage dumpster while she surveyed the situation. The two guards, both young men, were standing together under the security light, having a smoke and talking in quiet tones. Nancy silently climbed an access ladder leading to the low roof of the kitchen area and moved effortlessly to the roof's edge just above the men. The larger of the two men seemed to be telling a rather crude joke to the other guy. Just as they both chuckled at the punch line, Nancy leaped off the roof and landed directly behind them. She quickly landed a side kick to the knee of the larger man's left leg while almost simultaneously delivering an elbow strike to the smaller man's right temple. The smaller of the two men dropped like a rock, while the other man whimpered in pain as he grabbed his left knee, which now had a severely sprained medial collateral ligament. Nan followed the side kick to the knee of the first guard by executing a strike to his groin. The crotch strike not only caused excruciating pain but took his breath and prevented him from crying out. Nan quickly auto-injected both men with the sedative and waited in the shadows for Sonya and Kirk to show up.

After Sonya and Kirk arrived at the kitchen area, the three entered quietly through the door next to the loading dock using the access card Nancy had acquired from the downed senior guard. They continued wearing their MSS goggles, which doubled as night-vision goggles, as well as furnishing a location map for the interior of the building and the people in it. They crept past the large room containing the five sleeping guards and turned left into the holding area that contained Julianne. The single guard was sitting in a chair in front of the locked door containing Julianne. He appeared to be dozing and didn't make a sound when Sonya injected him with the tranquilizer. He slumped forward and was still.

Kirk placed a small amount of plasticized acid over the deadbolt lock and waited about thirty seconds before removing the lock core with a gripping screwdriver made for that purpose. The door creaked slightly as Nancy opened it, and she and Sonya entered the room where Julianne lay in the filthy prison bed. Kirk stayed outside the door to watch for trouble.

Nancy put her hand over Julianne's mouth and whispered, "Julianne, it's Nancy Choi. We've come to take you and your baby out of here."

"Oh, Nan, thank you so much! I've been bleeding, and I think my water may have broken...please help my baby live!" begged Julianne.

"Just be calm and quiet, Julianne. We've got to—"

Nancy's whispers were interrupted by a soft groan outside the door. Sonya opened the door, and they both saw Nancy's half-sister pulling the stiletto knife from Kirk's back. Before she could thrust it into Kirk's body again, Sonya charged Angel Jack and blocked the jumping front snap kick that Angel Jack threw at her head. Unfortunately, Sonya did not avoid the leg sweep and the slash to her thigh that Angel Jack delivered. Just as Angel Jack moved in for the kill, Sonya pulled off Angel Jack's goggles as Nancy turned on the bright overhead lights. Now temporarily blinded, Angel Jack had no defense for the bear claw strike Nancy delivered to her throat or the side kick to the solar plexus of the stunned assassin. As Angel Jack staggered into the rear wall, she managed to push the button on her left forearm that activated the alarm system. It only took a few seconds for the half-dressed guards to join the ruckus.

Sonya downed the first two men that rounded the corner with rapid fire from her APC automatic pistol. Even though Kirk was gravely wounded, he was able to get a round-off that caught the third guard in the neck. The last guards, a man and woman, pulled the gasping Angel Jack around the corner while laying down a barrage of automatic fire that pinned Nancy and Sonya in the room with Julianne.

Nancy pulled the critically injured Kirk into the room as Sonya returned fire. Once Kirk was inside,

Nancy closed and bolted the door. Sonya exposed the slash on her inner thigh, pulled the muscles together, and taped it shut with butterfly bandages followed by tissue glue. Then both women worked to stop the bleeding in Kirk's back. They could hear the wheezing from his punctured left lung as they packed the bloody hole with sterile gauze from the first aid kit Sonya was carrying and sealed the wound with tissue glue. Hopefully, that would keep him alive until they could reach real medical help. Nancy began to consider her options for escape when suddenly Julianne screamed, "The contractions have started! I think the baby is coming! Oh, God, please, please help us! Help us all!"

CHAPTER 7

Treason!

Clark didn't sleep that night. He had really messed things up this time. Not only had he deceived the whole American nation into starting two separate countries, but he had endangered the lives of his daughter and her precious son. Seth wasn't speaking to him. The prime ministers and other leaders were appalled and incredibly angry. His face was all over the news, where he was branded as a liar and traitor. A caricature had just shown up on the HV depicting him as a weasel holding a brass cross in one hand and a half-red-half-blue flag with the word "liar" emblazoned on it in the other hand.

Clark looked at the clock. It said 3:32 a.m. Clark rolled out of bed onto his knees and began to pray, "Lord, it's me, Clark.... I know we haven't talked much lately, but I really need Your help. I am so sorry for this mess I have made. I thought I was doing something that could help America, but in reality, I totally messed things up," said Clark softly.

Tears began to trickle down Clark's face as he continued to pray, "Lord, I don't care what happens to me...I just want Julianne and Little Clark to come home safely."

Now Clark began to sob, "I'm so sorry, Lord...I'm such an arrogant fool! I wave the Bible around like a weapon instead of a book declaring Your love. I have strayed so far from the fresh encounters I had right after I got to know You. Lord, I don't know what to say...I'm just a mess, and I've created chaos on so many levels. People are dead because of me. Please forgive me and help me be the man of God I'm supposed to be."

Clark stood up, shuffled into the den, and picked up his Bible. As he flipped it open, a verse in Psalm 51 caught his eye. Clark read it out loud, "'Create in me a clean heart, O God. Renew a loyal spirit within me.'[1] That's what I need, Lord...a clean heart and a right spirit..."

Clark began to sob and buried his face in his hands as he lay across the massive leather couch. Clark continued to cry and pray intermittently until he drifted off to sleep.

*****

Nancy looked at her watch. It was 4 a.m. The labor pains that Julianne had felt subsided, but she and the baby needed to get to the hospital. Now that Julianne's water had broken, the baby would come sooner rather than later, and that little one would need special care as a premature baby.

The patch job that Nancy and Sonya had done on Kirk seemed to be working as he was up and slowly moving about. Sonya had lost a little blood but was ready and eager to find a way out. As Nancy thought about these things, Kirk called out, "Hey, Admiral, take a look at this."

Nancy stepped around the corner and saw what Kirk had discovered. The return air duct was not welded shut but was fastened with security screws. They didn't have a security screwdriver, but they did have a good bit of Kirk's acid putty left.

"Here, Kirk, let me get that. We don't want to reopen your stab wound," said Sonya as she slid a small table under the vent.

Kirk handed the putty up to Sonya, who applied it to all eight security screws. In just a few seconds, the acid started sizzling as it ate its way into the metal. After a couple of minutes, Sonya was able to pull the return air register down, exposing a dark opening.

"Looks to be about 20x20," said Kirk. "A little small for me."

"I could never fit in that thing either," said Sonya. "I was cursed with my mama's wide hips. Looks like it's up to you, *Stretch*," Sonya said as she grinned at Nancy.

Nancy rolled her eyes while giving her friend a crooked smile.

Nancy stripped off her backpack, service belt, and chest protector. She took a vial of acid putty to use on the other end of the ductwork and strapped her 9mm handgun to her inner calf. There was no room for an assault rifle, so the handgun would have to do. She did manage to put two extra clips in her front shirt pockets. All three of them activated their communication devices, and then Kirk and Sonya boosted Nancy up into the duct.

Nancy inched her way along for about eight feet until she came to an intersection with the main return duct. The main duct was 48x36, which gave Nancy plenty of room to travel quickly. Nancy could hear a conversation a few feet in front of her, so she stopped to listen.

"I can't believe I let my brat half-sister get the jump on me like that," said Angel Jack in a very raspy voice. "She almost collapsed my windpipe with that strike. That witch is gonna pay with her life! So how many of us are left, anyway?"

"Just four are able to fight, including you, ma'am. The outside guards are alive but knocked out. I just left 'em in the yard," said a male voice with a thick European accent.

"Then four will have to be enough. We only have two to fight. I got my knife into that FBI guy rather well.

Check your ammo and make sure we have enough C-4 to take down the door to their room. I look forward to seeing the look in sweet princess Julianne's eyes when she sees me coming for her!" Angel Jack said before she began coughing violently.

Angel Jack's coughing fit gave Nancy time to scurry on past the room where the voices were coming from and reach the end of the return air duct. The large duct emptied into a huge air handler in the boiler room, but there was a sheet metal access door on the final horizontal run before the ductwork dropped into the air handling unit. Nancy used the acid putty to eat away the seams of the hinges and then pushed the access door onto the boiler room floor. She grabbed a metal ceiling joist and "hand walked" her way over to a mezzanine where she would only have to drop six feet.

Nancy contacted Sonya and Kirk via communicator and let them know that Angel Jack and her thugs were coming for them by blowing the door with a C-4 explosive. Sonya and Kirk moved Julianne to the back corner of the room and set up her bed and a couple of wooden pallets from the corner as a barricade against the automatic weapons fire that was sure to come. Julianne was groaning softly and praying as tears trickled down her cheeks.

"A little prayer wouldn't hurt us either," said Sonya.

"I've been praying ever since I felt that knife in my back," answered Kirk. "Actually, I've been asking the Father to give us all unusually clear minds and sharp aim."

"Will God answer a prayer that helps you kill another person? I thought the Bible said, 'Thou shalt not kill.'"[2] quizzed Sonya.

"Actually, a better translation would be 'Thou shalt do no murder.' There is a difference between killing to protect a woman and her unborn child from thugs and murdering an innocent person," stated Kirk.

"I see what you mean—so let's kill these guys as they come through the door, and we'll talk theology later," quipped Sonya.

*****

The knock at the door startled Clark, who was asleep on the couch. Clark looked at his watch and saw it was 5:31 a.m. He walked to the door and saw Seth standing alone. Clark opened the door, and Seth walked in slowly.

"Any news on our loved ones, Seth?" asked Clark.

"All I know at this point is that Admiral Choi thinks she knows where Julianne is and is attempting a rescue," answered Seth.

"Nancy's the best...if anyone can get your wife and the baby back, it's her.... Seth, I'm so sorry. This is all on me," moaned Clark.

"It was your idea, Clark, but I was with you every step of the way. I participated in everything except the charade regarding the extra nuclear devices. I still believe the Red-Blue scenario is the correct way to go," stated Seth.

"But I lied, Seth. I dismantled America based on a lie. If I hadn't forced Kennedy Watson's hand and dissolved his government, Julianne and the baby would be safe right now," said Clark.

"But if you hadn't forced his hand, Clark, we would still be stuck in the political mess that was America before the Red and Blue Nations came into being."

"So, where do we go from here, my friend?" asked Clark.

"That's what I want to talk to you about, Clark. If you surrender yourself to the Red prime minister and attorney general as a criminal, I believe Kennedy will release Julianne and the baby," offered Seth.

"What would be the charge?" queried Clark.

"Treason," said Seth.

"But treason is punishable by death in the Red Nation!" said a startled Clark.

"Right, but that is what Kennedy is demanding. Besides, you are a Red citizen," said Seth.

When Clark heard the words "treason" and "death," he trembled inside. He slowly walked to his desk, his place of authority and decision-making. After a few moments, he said, "Okay, Seth...I'll do it."

"I knew you would. That's why the Red Nation marshals are waiting for you downstairs in the main lobby. Gather a few personal things, and I'll walk you down. It will look better if you turn yourself in," said Seth.

* * * * *

The blast from the C-4 took the door right off its hinges and shoved it tight up against the barrier that Sonya and Kirk had made; however, Sonya, Kirk, and Julianne were not behind the barrier. Julianne had been hidden in a laundry storage closet with Sonya as her main guard, while Kirk had positioned himself behind Julianne's bed, where he covered himself with the mattress for protection from the blast.

"Kill the NBI agents but keep the girl alive!" shouted the lead mercenary soldier as he entered the room, spraying bullets at the barricade. As the smoke cleared a little, Kirk could make out the figure of the lead soldier and opened fire on him. As the soldier fell, the second man fired his automatic weapon into the mattress shielding Kirk. As the second soldier was firing at Kirk, Sonya burst from the laundry storage closet and shot him through the temple. The third mercenary scampered from the doorway in retreat toward Angel Jack, who was waiting in the hall corner.

Angel Jack was screaming hoarsely into her sat phone, "I don't care if Clark Johnson has confessed or not, Kennedy Watson. I am *going* to kill that little pregnant princess whether you authorize it or not!"

"What happened?" barked Angel Jack as she turned her attention to the lone mercenary.

"Thomas and Mustafa are down. The charge wasn't big enough to take out the door and kill the targets," said the mercenary.

"Well, that's no longer a problem. I've got enough C-4 in this duffel bag to blow the whole room off the end of the building and their whole team with it. You guard the door while I construct my little princess-killing super bomb," snarled Angel Jack.

The third mercenary took a position where he could see the door while Angel Jack put the bigger bomb together.

Sonya left Julianne momentarily to check on Kirk. She found him on the floor behind the mattress.

"Hey, *Rambo*, are you okay?" said Sonya while keeping one eye and her gun trained on the door.

"I think so.... The mattress slowed the bullets down, and my chest armor surprisedly stopped 'em well, but my forehead really stings. Can you tell me what's going on?" asked Kirk.

"Oh, I can tell you, all right...you've got a bullet sticking halfway into your forehead. The mattress must have slowed it down enough that your thick skull wouldn't let it travel into your brain," snickered Sonya.

"Gee, thanks for telling me. Can you pull it out?" asked Kirk.

"I could, but that might increase the bleeding. Right now, it's just sitting there...actually, it helps your looks," said Sonya with a smirk.

Kirk managed a smile and stood up slowly and said, "Let's check on the two mercenaries for signs of life."

Sonya checked Thomas and Mustafa while Kirk watched the hole where the door used to be. Thomas was dead while the other was bleeding badly but conscious.

"Please don't kill me...," Mustafa groaned. "I'm not a bad man...I just needed the money."

"Here, let me pack that chest wound," said Sonya.

"Don't bother...everything's getting dark...I guess I'm dying. Could you pray for me...?"

"I'm...sorry, soldier... I don't know how to pray," whispered Sonya.

The man gasped violently, grew totally still, and then slipped into eternity.

Nancy Choi had been listening from her position in the large air duct above Angel Jack's spot in the hall. There was a return air grille about two feet to the right. While Angel Jack was busy attaching the electronic ignition system and timer to the duffle bag full of C-4, Nancy slowly removed the filter and applied acid putty to the air grille hinges. As soon as the hinges gave way, Nancy dropped straight down from the ductwork as the grille crashed to the floor.

Angel Jack heard the hissing of the acid putty and was already facing Nancy when she landed in the hall.

"Why, sis, so good of you to drop in," said Angel Jack as she slashed at Nancy with her tactical spring-loaded stiletto.

"This isn't a social call, sister," quipped Nancy as she deflected the slashing knife with a quick side block and delivered a front snap kick to Angel Jack's solar plexus. As Angel Jack went down, her remaining soldier turned and fired at Nancy, striking her in the left thigh. He moved forward to finish Nancy off as she grabbed her thigh and dropped to her knees, but just as the soldier was taking aim at Nancy's chest, a shot rang out, and the soldier froze as his eyes glazed over. He fell right on top of Nancy and knocked her totally to the ground with his sheer body weight. Sonya ran over and rolled the mercenary off of Nancy.

"That's a pretty bad wound, Stretch. We've got to get a tourniquet on that very quickly," said Sonya in a concerned voice.

"Don't worry about me. Get Angel Jack," groaned Nancy.

"Let's take care of you first, Nan, then we'll take care of that murderous witch," asserted Sonya.

"Here, use this," Kirk said as he handed Sonya a ripped sheet from Julianne's bed to use as a tourniquet. "I'll go after Angel Jack."

While Sonya tightened the make-shift tourniquet above the wound on Nancy's thigh, Kirk moved cautiously down the hall toward the large door to the parking lot. Angel Jack was nowhere to be seen as she had used the shootings to escape. As Kirk reached the exit, he heard a loud whooshing sound. There, as dawn was breaking, Kirk saw Angel Jack's mini jet-copter rising into the early morning sky. He did manage to get off a few shots before she engaged the jet engine and streaked off into the new day, but Angel Jack was gone.

CHAPTER 8

Miracles and Mercenaries

When Kirk rejoined Sonya and Nancy in the hallway, he found them putting together a make-shift stretcher to carry Julianne out of the building.

"You ladies sure are working hard. Angel Jack is gone, and all her troops are neutralized. Can't we all take a breather?" asked Kirk with a happy voice.

"We could if Angel Jack hadn't started the timer on this bomb before she slipped away. Would you bring out Julianne and lay her in this stretcher and then go back and get our guns and backpacks? We've got...let's see...two minutes and forty-nine seconds. That's not enough time to disarm the device, but I believe we can be out and headed toward the hospital before this thing blows," said Nancy.

"Yes, ma'am, Admiral Choi! I'll get right on it!" said Kirk as he headed to pick up Julianne.

Nancy and Sonya finished the stretcher made of 1x4s from the pallets bound together with combat jackets they had removed from the fallen mercenaries. They didn't want to risk Julianne's contractions starting again if she attempted to walk. Kirk brought Julianne out of her former prison and gently laid her on the stretcher. She managed a weak smile and a soft "Thank you." Kirk went after the rest of their gear while Sonya and Nancy tended to Julianne.

"Here, sweetheart, drink this water. We have to keep you hydrated," said Sonya softly.

"Okay, let's move out," said Nancy.

"I'll slide the bomb behind the barricade in the detention room to deflect the explosion away from our direction. Then I'll catch up with you," said Kirk.

The two tired, limping women began to carry Julianne down the hall toward the north exit as fast as their wounds would allow. Kirk caught up with them and announced, "About thirty seconds."

The three commandoes and their precious cargo had just made it out of the doors when the bomb exploded. The blast blew the doors open and knocked all three rescuers to the ground. Nancy instinctively covered Julianne with her body. When the noise and the dust settled, Nancy asked, "Okay, who is the most mobile of you two?"

"I am!" they both answered simultaneously.

"Okay, Sonya has a severe leg injury, and Kirk was only stabbed in the back, so...we'll let Kirk go get the vehicle while 'we women folk' stay here with the pregnant lady," chuckled Nancy.

All three of them laughed, and Kirk trotted off after the vehicle.

Nancy activated her cell phone and made two quick calls. First, she called the local hospital and alerted them that three injured people and a woman in labor were about twenty minutes out. Then she called Seth.

"Nancy, I've been frantic. Did you rescue my wife and baby?" asked Seth.

"We've got them, Seth, and we are loading up to go to the local hospital now. We are all in pretty rough shape, but Julianne is holding up quite well. I'll call you again after we reach the hospital," said Nancy in a voice filled with fatigue.

"Thank you so much, Nan!" said Seth.

The three warriors and Julianne sped toward the hospital. A couple of Texas Highway patrol units met them halfway to their destination and escorted them to the hospital. Just as they pulled into the emergency room parking lot, Julianne shrieked, "The baby's coming! I feel his head against my hand!"

The medical team was waiting with a rolling stretcher to take her straight to delivery. Sonya and Kirk slowly got out of the car and described their wounds to attendants, who placed them in wheelchairs. In all the confusion, no one had immediately noticed that Nancy had not moved from behind the wheel.

Sonya blurted out, "Where's Nancy? Somebody, check the car for Admiral Choi."

An attendant opened the driver's side door, and Nancy slumped out of the car into his arms. She was not breathing.

*****

After Clark turned himself in to the Red Nation marshals, he was taken to the justice building, where he was arrested for treason against the Red Nation. Clark posted the $1,000,000 bond at the short hearing that followed and was released under house arrest.

Seth stayed with Clark during the whole process. The men had become closer during the last months as they worked together and shared the hope of a new son and grandson. Both men loved Julianne dearly, and the word of her rescue was great news. Then Seth got a phone call from the Athens, Texas, hospital.

"Mr. Goldstein, I'm Dr. Ruth Avery at the Athens General Hospital," said the doctor.

"Oh, doctor, thank you for calling. Has Julianne arrived yet?" asked Seth.

"Yes, she has, Mr. Goldstein, and she has given birth to your son. As you know, she went into labor in captivity, and the stress of that experience caused a great amount of trauma in both your wife and the baby," explained Dr. Avery.

"So, tell me, doctor; how are they?" asked Seth excitedly.

"Your wife is extremely exhausted from the kidnapping and delivery, but she should be fine. However, we are concerned about your son. Not only was he born prematurely, but we are detecting a heart murmur. We are arranging to airlift him to Houston as we speak," explained the doctor.

"Please do whatever is necessary to save our son! I will jet-copter out shortly to be with my wife. Thank you, doctor," said Seth.

Seth found Clark in the custody of the marshals and explained the whole situation to him.

"Seth, I am so sorry I can't travel to Athens with you... the marshals will transport me back to the compound in a few minutes. As you know, I'll be under house arrest until the trial. Again...I'm so sorry, son...this is all my fault," said Clark softly.

"This is not the time for one of your pity parties, Clark! Why don't you spend some time praying to that Jesus of yours? I need to go!" said Seth.

Seth gave Clark a quick hug and trotted off toward the parking lot.

* * * * *

Nancy awoke to a room full of doctors, nurses, technicians, and a crash cart.

"Who died?" mumbled Nancy.

"You did, Admiral Choi," said the lead doctor.

"Oh...I thought I just fainted from the blood loss," groaned Nancy.

"Actually, you died from blood loss. The bullet nicked your femoral artery, and the tourniquet couldn't stop the blood from pooling in your leg. We have restarted your heart, given you two units of blood, and repaired the artery. You are going to be just fine!"

"What about Julianne, Kirk, and Sonya?" asked Nancy.

Sonya and Kirk burst into the room, with Kirk pushing Sonya in a wheelchair.

"Hey Nan, you can ask us yourself!" said Sonya cheerfully as Kirk flashed a big smile.

"Okay, you two, out of here!" said the lead doctor. "I hate to kick out a couple of heroes, but Admiral Choi has been through a lot. Give her some time to rest, and then all three of you can catch up," said the doctor, as he slightly smiled and pointed toward the exit sign over the door.

Kirk asked for directions to the hospital cafeteria and rolled Sonya in that direction. After getting lost a couple of times, they found the cafeteria.

"Sorry to take you to eat hospital food, but I am famished!" exclaimed Kirk.

Sonya chuckled, "I'm hungry too. Saving the day and knocking off the bad guys can work up quite the appetite."

Kirk found an out-of-the-way table and parked Sonya in front of a large window. He took her order, went through the line, and paid for their food. After Kirk brought the tray piled high with fried chicken, mashed potatoes, and veggies, Sonya exclaimed, "I usually don't eat the fried stuff, but today is like a celebration. Give me one of those drumsticks!"

Kirk laughed as he saw Sonya chow down on the chicken leg. He helped himself to a breast with a huge scoop of mashed potatoes and stir fry on the side.

As Sonya dabbed her lips with a napkin, she said, "Hey Kirk, I've got a question."

"Sure, anything," mumbled Kirk through a mouthful of fried chicken.

"Well...it's just that...I'm in a wheelchair while my leg heals up, and Nan actually died for a little while, but you are moving around as if nothing happened to you. I know Angel Jack knifed you in the back, and I heard the air from your lung making a hissing sound as it came out of the hole in your back. I know we packed the wound and sealed it off with tissue glue, but you act like nothing is wrong with you. You're a pretty tough guy, but this is really amazing. What's going on, Kirk?"

"Well, Sonya, to be perfectly honest...the Lord healed me," said Kirk.

"The who did what?" exclaimed Sonya.

"That's what I said, Sonya. The Lord Jesus healed me," repeated Kirk slowly.

"Okay, Kirk, I know you got religion awhile back, but I'm being serious here. What *really* happened? I saw Angel Jack pull that seven-inch blade from your back and get ready to stick you again before Nan got to her. Plus, you could hardly walk after we dressed your wound," said Sonya with a puzzled look.

"That is what I am trying to say, Sonya. I was so weak and dizzy after I was stabbed that I knew I would be useless to you and Admiral Choi. So, I prayed and asked the Lord to heal me up so I could help you fight that evil bunch...and He did," said Kirk with a broad smile.

"Kirk...that's the most amazing thing I've ever heard of...I don't know what to say. You're telling me that God, uh Jesus, whatever...is real?" asked Sonya.

"That's exactly what I am saying, Sonya. God is real. Jesus is real. The Holy Spirit is real. The whole thing is real. Jesus really did die for the sins of the world, and He really does love us...you...all of us..." said Kirk.

Just then, a nurse from the ER approached their table and said with a loud voice, "Hey everybody, listen up! These are the two NBI agents that helped Admiral Choi save Julianne and her baby. I say we give them a big round of applause!"

The hospital personnel stood and clapped and cheered for the two heroes. Sonya and Kirk waved to everybody, and then Kirk began wheeling Sonya out of the cafeteria.

"I want to know more about this Jesus stuff, Kirk," said Sonya.

"I want to tell you all about it, Sonya. We'll get back together soon. Right now, let's check on Stretch."

"Ooh, don't let her hear you calling her by her nickname. I'm the only one that has that privilege," chuckled Sonya.

They both laughed and headed back to the ER wing. "So, how did Admiral Choi get the nickname Stretch?" inquired Kirk.

"It's a great story, Kirk. Nan was leading her SEAL team on a patrol in southern Syria. They had crossed into the outskirts of Basra when a roadside IED exploded and sent their Humvee careening toward a mountain ledge. An abrupt stop ejected a team member from the back seat and propelled him about six feet down the cliff. He managed to grab hold of some rocks and foliage, but his legs were dangling over the deep gorge below. Nancy became the bridge between his life and death. She told her master chief to grab her ankles and hold tightly while she slid off the ledge and stretched every fiber of her five-feet-ten-inch body, extending both hands toward the helpless SEAL. She pulled him up a few feet until the rest of the team could complete the rescue. From that moment on, she was affectionally known as Stretch Choi."

CHAPTER 9

Restoration

The jet-copter flight to Athens from Dallas was only about thirty minutes. It took Seth that long to drive to the Dallas Executive Airport from Clark's compound. Fortunately, the hospital would allow them to land on the Helipad. That would save an additional thirty minutes of car time. Seth settled into the passenger seat and leaned his head back for the short flight.

Seth's mind drifted back about five years ago to the first time he saw Julianne. Clark had invited Seth to the compound to share his ideas about the Red and Blue plan. Seth not only marveled at Clark's ingenious ideas but was in awe of his ministry compound. Clark and Seth had finished their first round of talks and were sitting on the second-floor veranda overlooking the back entrance. The afternoon was warm and breezy, with sun bathed ripples shimmering on the large lake behind the compound. As the two men enjoyed a glass of burgundy, a young woman could be seen jogging past the pier near the compound. Her slim but athletic body strode easily in the light breeze. The setting sun flashed orange highlights in her long auburn hair. Clark was droning on about some particular phase of his plan, but Seth was watching the girl.

"Seth, are you listening to me?" Clark asked with an agitated voice.

"Not really. I am looking at that amazing creature that is jogging in our direction," said Seth.

"That's no creature! That's my daughter Julianne!" laughed Clark. "She is quite lovely to look at. Julianne... so much like her mother. She also has a PhD in biology with an emphasis on computerization of biological systems. She finished at MIT two years ago and came to work for me here at the compound. Julianne is in charge of our laboratory and is already developing the biomedical tattoos that will be part of our identification plan when the Red and Blue Nations are established."

"Wow! Can I meet her?" asked Seth.

"Sure, as long as you keep your mitts off her! She will be up in a moment. She always has a big glass of green tea and vitamin water after her run," responded Clark.

Julianne appeared in a few minutes in her emerald green running tights and scooped neck beige overshirt with her tea and water mixture in a hydration flask. She opened the door to the veranda, expecting to see only her dad, and was startled to see Seth.

"Oh...Mr. Goldstein...hey...I've seen you on HV...I'm Julianne."

"Well, hello, Julianne. I've seen you running! Please, no more 'Mr. Goldstein'...I'm only thirty-two. Call me Seth."

Julianne smiled sheepishly, "Okay, and you can call me Julianne."

The pilot's voice broke into Seth's daydream, "Mr. Goldstein, we are beginning our descent. Please fasten your seatbelt and make sure your seat is in the upright position."

*****

Clark was all alone in his suite at the compound. He was wearing an ankle bracelet that would send an electronic signal to the guard outside his door if he attempted to leave the suite, or even raised a window. He wondered about Julianne and the baby but knew Seth would call him when he received any news.

Clark's mind drifted back to the early days of his ministry. He had been so full of love for God and people. The happy marriage with his pretty young wife was so sweet, and he felt like he was making a difference in the world. Clark actually felt that he was in the cradle of God's hand.

Clark had especially been drawn to prisoners. Much of his early ministry had been in jails and prisons. He used to jokingly say, "Well, the offerings aren't very good, but at least I've got a captive audience." After he became a full-time pastor, he still did volunteer work with the incarcerated—men like himself that had grown up poor, afraid, and insecure—men that had no fathers in their lives.

Then the success of larger churches and bigger salaries took over his life. Clark began to operate more in his own strengths and giftings and less in God's promptings. His fiery preaching and amazing likeability led to the establishment of his HV ministry and huge influence in the country. Then, with the Christian Nationalist mission theme in tow, it was just a matter of time until he could make the right contacts to institute his Red Nation Blue Nation solution to a divided United States of America. Clark was trying to be the father he never had to a nation of 380 million people—and he did it by force and deceit.

Clark snickered when he thought of the many hours of ministry he enjoyed while sharing with prisoners in orange jumpsuits. Now it looked like he would be dangling at the end of a rope in his own stained orange jumpsuit. Still...God always made a way of escape.

Clark went over to his wine closet and poured himself a quarter glass of burgundy. He then went to the pantry and pulled out a single saltine cracker. Clark approached the little desk in the sitting room, placed the wine and cracker on the desktop, and pulled one of his many Bibles off the bookcase above the desk. He found a passage in 1 Corinthians 11 and began to read it out loud,

> "This is my body, which is given for you. Do this in remembrance of me." In the same way, he took the cup of wine after supper, saying, "This cup is the new covenant between God and his people—an agreement confirmed with my blood. Do this in remembrance of me as often as you drink it." ...So anyone who eats this bread or drinks this cup of the Lord unworthily is guilty of sinning against the body and blood of the Lord. That is why you should examine yourself before eating the bread and drinking the cup. For if you eat the bread or drink the cup without honoring the body of Christ, you are eating and drinking God's judgment upon yourself.[3]

Clark closed the Bible and got down on his knees in front of the little desk. "Lord, it's me, Clark. We haven't talked in a while. I've been so busy doing Your work, or so I thought, I have neglected our relationship. I've dishonored Your body and Your blood, and I realize that I am under Your judgment. My failure to really love You and serve You has brought nothing but trouble to me, my family, and our nation.... Lord, I am so sorry. I have whined when I should have prayed and lied to the people You entrusted me with. Please forgive me for my pride, Jesus! Please forgive every sin by Your mercy! Please restore me, Lord, and make me the man You want me to be."

Clark then reached up to the desk and brought the wine and saltine cracker close to him. He blessed them both, set the wine down, and broke the cracker. "I receive Your broken body, Lord, for my healing and wholeness." Clark ate the cracker and then lifted the wine glass off the floor.

The wine swirled in the clear goblet as if it were alive. "Lord Jesus, this is Your blood that was spilled out for me—my salvation and the cleansing of my sins. I receive it in Your presence." Clark took a sip of wine, and it was sweet to his taste. How could something so simple bring such a profound sense of peace? Clark stood to his feet. "Thank You, Father God, for forgiving me. Thank You, Jesus, for saving me, and thank You, Holy Spirit, for once again empowering me. Praise God!" Clark settled onto his oversized sofa for an undetermined amount of time, and he rested. Years of strife and competition slid off every fiber of Clark's being. He felt like a new man with a new covenant.

*****

With Clark, Seth, and Nancy all indisposed, the Red Blue Leadership Team met in an emergency session with only three senior members plus the various aides and legal minds that actually did most of the work.

Leon Brown spoke up first, "So, what is the state of the Red and Blue Nations after Clark revealed his deception?"

A female research analyst replied, "Actually, sir, all of our polling shows that the two countries have not reacted with violence, protest, or much excitement upon hearing the news of Clark's treachery. In fact, 90 percent of the citizens of the Red and 70 percent of the Blue seem to be more interested in their own affairs rather than what has recently transpired. Of course, the major news networks are calling for investigations and a public trial for Clark, but no one seems to care. Amazingly enough, people are more interested in Julianne's rescue and the fate of her baby."

"Well, that is amazing...and a bit troubling..." said Blue Prime Minister Maria Cortez.

"Why is it troubling, Maria? Clark was arrested by the Red Nation for treason against the Red Nation. What does it have to do with you or your liberal followers?" asked Red Prime Minister Sikes with a sarcastic grin.

"It's just that what he did is *wrong*, Charles," Maria said as she raised her voice.

"But it's no more wrong than your approval of the death of millions of aborted babies!" Charles shot back.

"Now, wait a minute, you two!" Leon Brown said with a curt, sharp voice. "Your personal opinions and vendettas have no place here. Our job is to make decisions that allow both nations to flourish in their own chosen political and governmental styles. We are through trying to change each other, remember?"

"Yeah, you're right.... Sorry, Leon...sorry, Maria," groaned Charles. Maria ignored the apology and stared straight ahead.

Leon then asked for a legal opinion on Clark's status from the team's chief legal aid, Marcus Thorn. Thorn shuffled through some files, adjusted his laptop, and then cleared his voice to speak, "Mr. Brown, ladies, and gentlemen...I have some interesting news to reveal to you. We have researched the charges against Clark Johnson and recommend that all charges be dropped."

"What do you mean, drop the charges?" Maria hissed.

"Yeah, everybody saw exactly what Clark did—the lies and the deceit. Even though Clark is my friend, he is not above the law," stated Charles with a confused look on his face.

Leon beckoned for Mr. Thorn to continue. Thorn cleared his throat again, adjusted his glasses, and once more began to speak, "Clark Johnson cannot ever be charged for treason against the Red Nation or the Blue Nation. When Clark set off the first nuclear blast on an uninhabited island and lied about having additional devices in major cities, he did so before the Red Nation and Blue Nation existed. Plus, the United States of America does not exist anymore, so his crimes are null and void. About the only thing anyone could do is hit him with a class action civil suit brought by former citizens of a now defunct nation. I really don't see that happening... do you?"

The group sat in shocked silence for a second or two, and then Leon Brown started chuckling.

Charles and the legal team joined in the laugh while Maria stewed. A few hours later, the Red Nation attorney general personally went to Clark's compound to let him know that all charges had been dropped and that Clark was free to rejoin the RBMT as its leader. Clark smiled broadly as the marshal removed the house arrest monitoring system from his ankle. As soon as the men left, Clark called his driver. He was going to see his grandson.

CHAPTER 10

Big Foot

Seth sat on the corner of Julianne's hospital bed and held her for a long time. Neither one of them spoke. They just drew courage and strength from each other. Finally, Julianne whispered, "I love you, Seth. We will make it through this, and our son will be fine."

"I hope you're right, sweetheart," sighed Seth.

"I know I'm right, darling…. God rescued me from Angel Jack, and He will take care of little Clark. Prayer plus good medical treatment is unbeatable," said Julianne with a perky grin.

The charge nurse came in with a clipboard and announced, "Okay, Mr. and Mrs. Goldstein, you are cleared to jet-copter to Houston to be with your son. You must have one of our medical techs go with you to ensure that Mrs. Goldstein has no post-delivery problems while you are en route. If you will each sign these release forms, you can leave in about an hour…and by the way, it's been a pleasure serving you."

"Thank you so much, Nurse Hobbs. You and the staff have been wonderful!" said Julianne with her now sparkling smile. After the nurse left, Julianne said, "Seth, honey, there is one thing we need to do before we leave. We must see Admiral Choi, Sonya, and Kirk. They saved my life and almost lost theirs doing so. I must thank them personally."

"Of course, sweetheart, I certainly want to thank them too. After all, they saved my greatest treasure," said Seth as tears formed in his eyes.

Just as Seth leaned over to give Julianne a kiss, the threesome burst into the room with big grins and friendly greetings. Admiral Choi was in a wheelchair sporting a pink hospital gown while Sonya, dressed in her tee-shirt and combat pants, was using a walking cane. Kirk was in his full battle uniform, minus the body armor. He said he would have worn his tee-shirt, but it "stunk too bad."

Seth immediately hugged Nancy Choi and then shook hands with Sonya and Kirk. "You three will never know how grateful I am for your rescuing Julianne and the baby. You are heroes, and I will be in your debt forever," said Seth.

"There's no debt to be owed, Seth. Not only was our mission a labor of love, but also an opportunity to serve both the Red and Blue Nations. We are extremely glad we were successful," declared Nancy.

"Yeah, we only wish we had successfully apprehended Angel Jack," chimed in Sonya.

"But we did destroy her base and take down the group of mercenaries that worked with her, so not a bad day's work!" Kirk said with a grin.

"But tell us about your son," said Nancy.

"Well, he's been air-lifted to the Dallas Prenatal Unit, and his vitals are stable...but he was born with a pneumothorax and heart murmur," said Julianne before she choked up and couldn't continue.

Seth resumed Julianne's narrative, "A pneumothorax is caused by a pinhole in the bronchial tube that allows air to escape into the baby's chest cavity where it puts pressure on his heart. The doctors in Dallas have already done a simple procedure, inserting a chest tube causing negative pressure that allows the pneumothorax to heal with time. He should be fine. We are so grateful and anxious to see him. The doctors have cleared Julianne to fly, so we are leaving soon."

"But we weren't leaving before we saw our heroes!" exclaimed Julianne.

"Well, you've seen us. So hit the road...I mean the air!" laughed Kirk. "Oh, and I'll be praying for all three of you," he added.

"Actually, we all will," said Sonya in a quiet voice. Nancy nodded in agreement.

After a few more hugs, the heroes left.

Julianne dressed in the new outfit and undergarments the Athens Hospital nurses had bought her. Seth disposed of her old, battered running outfit she had worn before the kidnapping last week. Julianne and Seth said goodbye to the staff and headed for the helipad accompanied by the med-tech that would monitor Julianne's condition on the short jet-copter flight to Dallas. They were off to see Little Clark!

* * * * *

Angel Jack landed her mini jet-copter on the helipad reserved for Kennedy Watson's personal aircraft. As the whine of the turbine engines died down, Angel Jack's thoughts of the past two hours about her teenage years came to a conclusion.

At Calvary Catholic High School, when she was still known as Angelica, she had been such a tall, lanky girl that the other kids made fun of her unmercifully. Plus, she was not particularly attractive, with her angular features and big feet.

Angelica was certainly not going to get any invitations to the homecoming dance. The basketball coach had noticed her tall frame and asked her to join the team, but she had no desire to participate in team sports. She did, however, begin taking Taekwondo classes at the age of thirteen. Her instructor, Mr. Sun, was a ninth-degree Korean black belt who was "old school" in his approach to teaching his students martial arts. Mr. Sun noticed immediately that Angelica was extremely quick for a large girl. Angelica advanced in her martial arts skills at an amazing rate. She earned her first-degree black belt by the age of sixteen and continued to work tirelessly to learn the kicks, punches, and grappling moves that would help define her career in later years. Angelica would work with Mr. Sun after class to learn advanced techniques. Plus, the martial arts classes would get her out of the house and away from the parents she despised. Both of her parents drank heavily, and the screams and shouts from their frequent fights had brought the police to their house on several occasions.

A couple of weeks before Angelica was scheduled to graduate from Calvary Catholic High, a male student named Mack purposefully tripped her in the lunchroom. Angelica fell onto a table and spilled her lunch all over the head cheerleader. "Watch it, freak!" screamed the cheerleader.

The laughter began quietly and then crescendoed through the whole cafeteria. After Angelica picked herself up, the boy who had tripped her said, "Hey clumsy, did those big feet get in your way?"

Angelica paused and angrily glared at Mack. He pulled a large pocketknife and tauntingly said, "Hey Big Foot, I heard you know how to defend yourself. Let's see whatcha got!" The boy playfully lunged at Angelica with the three-inch blade, and before she even considered how to respond, her training kicked in.

Mr. Sun had always taught his students that martial arts were defensive in nature but could be used aggressively in case of real danger. Angelica considered this knife attack real danger, especially since it was accompanied by jeers from the other students. Angelica sidestepped the knife, then grabbed Mack's fist with both her hands and twisted it away from his body and downward. The boy yelped, dropped the knife, and then remembered nothing else as Angelica's right knee crushed his nose and sinus cavities. The boy hit the tile floor with a thud and lay motionless as blood from his nose pooled under his head. Angelica assumed her fighting stance and said slowly while surveying the crowd, "Anyone else care to try the *freak*?"

Even though the boy had attacked Angelica first, her response was deemed highly inappropriate, and she was dismissed from school before her graduation. Mack recovered, but his nose was never quite right after the incident. Angelica's French father and American mother were livid because of the fight and embarrassed that she would not graduate. They kicked her out of the house ten days before her eighteenth birthday. Her drunk father threw her clothes in the front yard and cursed her in French as she walked away. There was nowhere else to go except the dojo. Mr. Sun had given

Angelica a key to the building because she taught some of the classes in his absence, so at least she would have a roof over her head.

Angelica walked the two miles to the dojo, entered through the back door, and found a mat to sleep on. She cried herself to sleep that night but swore through her tears that no one would ever make fun of her or mistreat her again. One day's events had formed the paradigm Angelica would live by for the rest of her life. Everyone that crossed her would pay dearly! She was now Angel Jack!

Angel Jack's thoughts returned to the present as the engine shut completely down. It was time to attend to the task at hand. She strode into the lobby and checked her 9mm sidearm and her infamous stiletto knife with the guards at the entrance to the Cavalier Hotel's executive suite.

Kennedy Watson's family had owned property at Martha's Vineyard for over fifty years, and the Cavalier Hotel had been built by Kennedy's father about fifteen years ago. The hotel served as an overflow for guests visiting the Martha's Vineyard area as well as a networking location for Kennedy's administrative group.

Angel Jack strode into Kennedy Watson's large private office accompanied by two armed guards. Kennedy was alone and sporting a huge grin. "We took her weapons and patted her down, sir. She also cleared the metal detector...she is clean," said the younger guard.

"Okay, Tony, but please stay with us until this meeting is over," said Kennedy in a non-threatening voice. "We welcome the world's greatest assassin! Please be seated, Angel Jack," Kennedy said sarcastically.

"I prefer to stand...where's the rest of my money, Kennedy?" Angel Jack coldly asked.

"You'll get the rest of your money when you finish the job, sweetheart," Kennedy smirked.

"Okay, Kennedy, I don't have time to deal with your shenanigans. You specifically promised me $500,000 for the kidnapping and another $500,000 when Clark confessed his deception publicly. Both of those things have happened. I want to be paid...now!" said Angel Jack with her raspy voice rising.

Watson shifted in his chair and took a sip of water. "Do you not remember my telling you to terminate Julianne after Nancy Choi and her team attempted to rescue her?" asked Kennedy Watson with a sneer.

"Of course, I remember you saying that, Kennedy, but that wasn't our initial deal. I decided to kill the little princess, but that act was on my own. Termination has always cost you two million dollars for a high-profile person like Julianne Goldstein. You paid the same assassination fee several times during your presidency. I am tired of talking about this, Kennedy. Transfer the final $500,000 to my offshore account now, or you will regret it eternally," said Angel Jack in a low, quiet voice.

The two security guards put their hands on the butts of their sidearms as Kennedy threw his head back and laughed heartily.

"What are you going to do, sweetheart? Talk me to death?" Kennedy trilled.

Suddenly Angel Jack snatched the poison-tipped acrylic throwing star from her hair and threw it side-armed into the soft tissue of Kennedy's neck. Then Angel Jack side kicked the guard to her right in the solar plexus, spun the back of her body into his chest, and captured his drawn gun with a wrist and forearm lock. Using the guard's gun, she shot the second guard in the chest as he was drawing his weapon. As the wounded guard slumped to the floor, Angel Jack then used the gun of the guard she was controlling and shot him in the forehead. Angel Jack locked the office door and said as she approached the dying Kennedy Watson, "Transfer the money now, Kennedy, and I'll give you the antidote to my poison-tipped star."

Watson slowly typed in his banking password while making gurgling sounds as blood and saliva dribbled from his mouth. He slowly made a few more strokes on his keyboard and said in a weak, gravelly voice, "There... it's done...see for yourself...check your account."

Angel Jack logged into her account on her hand-held device and said, "Well, congratulations Kennedy. You are a man of your word...at least when you are dying?"

"Please.... I did what you said...please...the antidote," rattled Kennedy.

"Gee...I think I forgot the antidote after all. Sorry about that, Kennedy. I guess I'll see you in hell!" said Angel Jack with a wicked grin.

Kennedy let out a half-gurgle-half-gasp and slumped forward onto his desk.

The panoramic window behind Kennedy's slumping dead body provided the perfect escape route for the now-enriched assassin. Angel Jack broke the decorative window glass with an elbow strike and rappelled down the backside of the office complex. She waited at the building's corner as the other security guards and employees smashed open the door to Kennedy's office suite. After a few moments delay, Angel Jack simply entered the empty foyer, retrieved her favorite Smith and Wesson 9mm handgun along with her Italian stiletto knife, and quickly headed for the helipad.

The horrified staff and guards discovered the now dead Kennedy Watson and two security guards, but there was nothing to be done. They watched helplessly through the broken window as Angel Jack's mini copter quickly sped away.

*****

Clark Johnson peered through the large glass window at the viewing area of the Neonatal ICU at his grandson

Clark Seth Goldstein and whispered a prayer for the little infant. He looked so small and helpless, with tubes and IVs coming out of his tiny body. The head nurse had assured him that the procedure to correct the pneumothorax had gone well and that baby Clark should be home in a few weeks. Clark was so very thankful. He was just about to quiz the nurse on a few items when Seth and Julianne walked into the viewing area.

"Oh, Daddy, it's so good to see you!" squealed Julianne as she hugged Clark tightly.

Seth grabbed Clark's free hand with a firm, friendly shake and said, "Hey, Granddad, I heard you beat the treason rap. You never cease to amaze me, Clark Johnson!"

Clark chuckled and said, "Well, we do serve a forgiving God...plus, good lawyers don't hurt either."

Julianne asked the nurse if it would be possible for her to hold Little Clark and was told that it was a little early for personal contact. However, the nurse did give Julianne a breast pump and asked her to "get the boy some supper." Julianne was ushered to a room for nursing mothers and shown how to use the breast pump. Little Clark had been on formula since his birth, but the nurse said that his mom's milk would be the best thing for him. Julianne was delighted to nourish her son, even if it was through a bottle of pumped breast milk at the neonatal ICU.

While Julianne worked on Little Clark's dinner, Clark and Seth chatted in the waiting room. Mostly their talk was "father-grandfather business" until Seth's cell phone rang, and he said,

"It's Leon; I better take the call.... Hello, Leon. Yes, we're at the hospital now. Little Clark is doing fine and should be home in a few weeks. Yes...Julianne is recovering nicely...so what's up, my friend? You are kidding... Angel Jack killed Kennedy Watson...oh my God!" Seth put the phone on speaker so Clark could hear while Leon gave the details of the assassin's strike. After Leon hung up, Seth looked directly at Clark and stated, "We've got to get that murderous witch, Clark. I believe we should set up a joint task force manned by both Red and Blue agents to find and capture Angel Jack.

"I totally agree, Seth...but let's try her under Red law... that way, we can publicly hang her!" said Clark through clenched teeth.

After Julianne finished pumping her breast milk, all three waved goodbye to the baby through the glass barrier and went their separate ways. Julianne checked into a nursing mothers' suite so she could furnish breast milk for Little Clark on a regular basis. Seth planned to go by their home and pick up clothes and personal items for Julianne and bring them back to the hospital. Clark's driver and personal bodyguard met him in the main lobby to drive him back to the compound. Clark prayed silently during the ride, "Thank You, Lord, for saving Julianne and Little Clark. Lord, I ask You to bless Seth. He's a good man and loves his family. And Lord... thank You so much for giving me another opportunity to show people that I really am a man of God."

*****

Nancy, Sonya, and Kirk took their time as they savored the delicious peach cobbler that had topped off their meal of fried chicken and fresh vegetables. They had gone straight to the same little diner outside of town after their hospital release was processed. Even though all three worked in the D. C. area, they couldn't pass up a great Southern meal.

"Aw man, I think I got my fill of grease and sugar," said Kirk as he smacked his lips.

"Don't forget the cholesterol. I'll bet mine went up fifty points!" laughed Nancy.

"Come on, Stretch, I'll bet you didn't gain a pound during this whole week of inactivity in the hospital," teased Sonya.

"Well, if I did, I'll work it off when I get back home," said Nancy with a wink.

"Well, before we do head for home, Kirk needs to tell us about this 'Jesus stuff,'" quipped Sonya.

"Right, what's this about your being healed from that deep knife wound?" asked Nancy with an inquisitive look.

"Okay, ladies, mind if I start at the beginning?" asked Kirk. Nancy and Sonya both nodded in the affirmative, and Kirk continued, "About three years ago, I attended a special weapons training seminar put on by the bureau. My roommate was a guy named Jamie Reynolds, with the FBI task force that works out of the Kansas City office. Really nice guy and a heck of an agent. One night before we turned in, I noticed him reading a big leather-bound book and asked him what he was reading. He said that the big book was his study Bible and that he was reading from the book of John. I had certainly seen a Bible. My parents were atheists, but my grandfather on my mom's side, a particularly good and gentle man, read his Bible when I spent the night at his house. He even read to me a little bit and would say prayers with me before bedtime. That was something my parents never did. Anyway, this guy Jamie asked me if I knew Jesus. I said that I knew who Jesus claimed to be, but I didn't understand how I could know someone who lived over 2000 years ago. Then Jamie astounded me by saying that Jesus really did rise from the dead and lives in the hearts of those who believed in Him."

Sonya interrupted, "So you are saying that Jesus is real and lives inside of you?"

"Well, not at first," Kirk continued. "Jamie explained to me that mankind was separated from God by sin, but Jesus came to bridge the gap by giving His life as a payment for the sins of the world. I really need to show you some scriptures if that is all right with you two."

"It's fine with me," said Sonya. "I saw Angel Jack stick that big knife in your lung and heard the air escaping from the wound when we dressed it. But you didn't die; you got perfectly well really quickly. That was a miracle, and if Jesus did it, I want to know all about it! Okay?"

Nancy had been listening quietly while Kirk told his story, but now she spoke up, "I've heard about Jesus before and actually believe in Him. I just don't talk about it. I was raised Catholic and went to mass as a kid. I never finished confirmation classes, but I did accept Jesus as Savior at a youth retreat when I was fourteen. I guess I just kind of lost touch with spiritual things as my career progressed."

"You are a Christian? Are you kidding me, Nancy?" exclaimed an astonished Sonya.

"I guess I am, Sonya," said Nancy. "I honestly believe that Jesus is God's Son and died for the sins of the world...I just don't know much more than that. Come on, Kirk, and show us the scriptures. We need to hear them."

Kirk continued as he went to a Bible app on his phone and opened a three-way communication link. Kirk sent a copy of Romans 3:23 to both women and read the verse out loud, "'For everyone has sinned; we all fall short of God's glorious standard.' This verse says that all of us are sinners. Do both of you agree that you are sinners?"

"Hell yes! I know I am!" said Sonya quickly as Nancy nodded in the affirmative.

Kirk continued, "Unfortunately, sin has consequences. Romans 6:23 says that the wages or payment for sin is death. We all die physically, but this verse is talking about a spiritual death where we are separated from God forever."

Nancy interjected, "You're talking about hell, right?"

"Right," Kirk continued. "But no one has to go to hell. The rest of Romans 6:23 says that the gift of God is eternal life through Jesus Christ our Lord. Jesus' death on the cross paid our sin debt."

"Oh my God, you're telling me that all this stuff is real?" Sonya moaned.

"It's all real, Sonya. Jesus is real, heaven is real, hell is real," said Kirk. "You know it's true in your heart...plus there is my miraculous healing from the lung puncture. Jesus did that because He loves us all and answered my request for healing so I could do my job on our rescue squad."

"This is utterly amazing. I thought God and Jesus were too busy running the universe to answer specific prayers by everyday people...amazing," said Nancy softly as tears formed in her brown eyes.

"Okay, what you're saying is hitting me hard, but this has the ring of truth...so what is the next step for us sinners? I guess I'll have to change my ways," mumbled Sonya.

"A lot of people think that's what God wants, but that won't get the job done. Let me ask you a question, Sonya...have you ever been fishing?" asked Kirk.

"You know I have! We went on that company deep sea fishing trip together and caught a mess of fish. Then we cooked 'em up. Tasty!" exclaimed Sonya.

"So, here's my question, Sonya. Did we clean the fish before we caught 'em or after?" Kirk asked with a big grin.

Sonya lifted one eyebrow, smirked, and said, "After, of course, smart guy."

"Well, that's the way Jesus is too.... He cleans you up after He catches you. You give Him your heart and make Him boss of your life, and then He gives you eternal salvation and starts the cleaning process simultaneously," said Kirk.

"That's what was missing for me!" Nancy said in almost a shout. "I believed in Jesus but never thought I could be good enough that He would actually want to be with me."

"My pastor puts it this way," said Kirk. "God is not looking for perfection...He's looking for connection. God loves us and wants to bless us in every area of our lives."

Sonya interrupted, "I'm all in, Preacher Kirk; how do we make this happen?"

Kirk continued, "It's actually quite simple. Romans 10:9–10 puts it this way,

> If you openly declare that Jesus is Lord and believe in your heart that God raised him from the dead, you will be saved. For it is by believing in your heart that you are made right with God, and it is by openly declaring your faith that you are saved.

"Would you ladies like to make a decision to receive His forgiveness and make Jesus the Lord of your lives?"

"I definitely would," said Nancy. "I believe that Jesus is real, but never knew that He wanted to know me personally. This is such good news!"

Sonya chimed in, "Oh, yeah, I need someone to fix my messed-up life! Let's do it!"

"Okay, friends," said Kirk as he took both their hands, "pray this simple prayer to Jesus after me. 'Lord Jesus...I come to You as a sinner...I know that I deserve death and hell for my sins...but I don't want to die and be separated from You...I ask You to forgive me of all my sins and take charge of my life...I turn away from sin and choose You as the boss of my life...thank You, Jesus, for saving me...amen!'"

After a silent moment that hung heavy with the Spirit of God, Kirk prayed for his new sisters in Christ, "Father, I thank You so much for my new sisters that have joined our family. I ask You to protect them and fill them with Your Holy Spirit. Amen!"

Sonya gave Kirk a high five and said with a huge grin, "This is awesome! I feel so clean inside! Thank You, Jesus, and thank You, brother Kirk!"

Admiral Nancy Choi just put her head in her hands and wept as she whispered, "Thank You so much, Lord... I just didn't know how much You loved me...thank You... thank You."

Kirk responded, "Thank you, ladies. It was an honor to pray with you."

CHAPTER 11

The Misfits

Clark sat in the big, paneled boardroom in his Christian National Compound and had a second cup of morning coffee. The rest of the RBMT would get to the meeting about thirty minutes later.

Clark's mind roamed around the events of the last couple of weeks, as well as thinking back to his married life with his now-deceased wife. Clark met Olivia while they were both students at Dallas Theological Seminary. Olivia had a real desire to go to the foreign mission field, while Clark wanted to become a pastor in the States. Clark thought about the first time he had seen Olivia. She was walking down the stairs at the student union building with a group of other students. When Clark saw her, he froze in his tracks. Her long brown hair and blue eyes captivated him. She was not tall, about five feet five inches, but her perfect figure and tinkling laugh were mesmerizing. Who was this young, beautiful Christian woman? Clark knew that he might never see her again and decided to act. He bumped into her on purpose and spilled his latte on her forearm and books.

"Ouch...that's hot!" shrieked Olivia Moore.

"I am so sorry," lied Clark. "Here, let me clean that up...I am so deeply sorry."

"Oh, it's okay. You didn't get my laptop, so everything's good," said Olivia.

"Again...I am so sorry...uh...my name is Clark Johnson," said Clark with his best and biggest smile.

"I'm Olivia Moore, and I know who you are. I heard you present that senior paper on Christian nationalism last week at the convocation," said Olivia with a gentle smile.

"Oh, really...was it any good?" asked Clark sheepishly.

"It wasn't too bad," Olivia teased. "Hey, I've got to get to my New Testament Greek class. See you around, Clark Johnson."

Clark sputtered, "Hey...uh...would you have coffee with me this afternoon if I promise not to spill it on you? We could meet at Poppi's Coffee House."

"I think that could be arranged...I'll be sure and wear something that I wouldn't mind getting coffee stains on," said Olivia with a giggle.

Clark's thoughts were interrupted as the door opened, and Admiral Nancy Choi strode in with her two assistants. She was dressed in her formal navy-blue suit. Her medals were on full display, and her admiral rank pin was attached to her collar. Clark immediately stood and gave Nancy a tight hug. "Nancy, I know I told you on the phone several times, but I wanted to say in person how incredibly grateful I am to you and your team for saving Julianne and Little Clark. You are truly an amazing friend!" Clark said sincerely.

"Of course, Clark...it was my pleasure to serve you and your family. May I introduce the other members of our rescue squad? This is Sonya Arthur and Kirk Waters. I wrestled them away from the former FBI and made them my two top assistants for our RBMT," Nancy said with a sly grin.

"That is wonderful," said Clark as he extended both his hands to Kirk and Sonya. "I am so grateful to both of you for saving Julianne and Little Clark. If there is anything I can do for either of you, please let me know."

Sonya and Kirk took their seats behind Admiral Choi as she settled in at the big boardroom table. The other team members and assistants filed in over the next few minutes, and Clark's executive assistant cued in the agenda to the multiple holo stations at 8:30 a.m. sharp.

Seth opened the meeting by personally thanking Nancy, Sonya, and Kirk for saving his family and then took up the first item on the agenda, which read: Blue Nation Failing.

"As you know," said Seth, "the Blue Nation has once again fallen behind on its debts, and the World Bank refuses to loan them any more money without raising the interest rate by an additional two percentage points. Maria, would you like to enlighten us with the details?"

Maria Cortez was wearing her power colors today. Her bright red business suit, diamond stud earrings, and a simple gold chain with a diamond and sapphire pendant completed her outfit. She stood quickly and began speaking as she looked directly at Clark, "My friends, the Blue Nation is in trouble. Our economy is growing by only 1.2 percent, and our unemployment rate has soared to 11 percent. Over 30 percent of our people are receiving government assistance, and the number of Blue citizens in jail or prison is double that of the Red Nation. I have argued with my Red counterparts about the need for social services for all but to no avail. These problems are financially breaking our country. Therefore, I humble myself before you today and ask for your guidance." The tears in Maria's eyes turned into a gushing torrent as she broke down before the entire group. Seth and Clark were the first ones to her. Both men attempted to comfort Maria by placing their hands on her shoulders, but she buried her head into Seth's chest and continued to sob as she moaned, "I don't know what to do...I don't know what to do...." Her stunned aides glanced back and forth at each other before joining the wailing Maria to offer comfort.

Charles Sikes, the Red prime minister, spoke up as the crying and comforting continued, "Did anyone not see this coming? History has proven that all forms of liberalism, whether communism or Maria's Blue Nation brand of socialism, always lead to low productivity, government dependence, and low self-esteem. Her Blue people don't need to work; they get it all given to them."

Seth pried Maria loose from his chest as he spoke up sharply, "Knock it off, Charles! Can't you see that she is hurting? I'll be the first to admit that our Blue Nation needs tweaking, but at least we haven't done 3,800 public hangings over the last two years."

"Right, you haven't executed anybody! All your drug dealers and murderers are in prison, costing your Blue taxpayers $200,000 a year per prisoner. No wonder you are broke!" Charles shot back.

Clark spoke up, "Friends, I believe I know how to solve our dilemma." Clark continued with a quivering voice, "I believe we ought to reestablish the United States of America."

"What? Have you lost your mind?" said Charles with an incredulous look. "We have political utopia in the Red Nation. We have less than 2 percent unemployment and greatly reduced crime against Red citizens. We are paying our part of the national debt down and operate on a balanced budget. Our industries are thriving, and the divorce rate is down to only 25 percent. Why would we want to unequally yoke ourselves up with the same people that have held us back with their oppressive laws and regulations?"

"I agree with Clark," said Leon Brown. "We need the compassion that the Blue Nation exhibits to the less fortunate and the drive and business acumen of the Red Nation."

"Over my dead body!" Charles bellowed.

Seth stood and raised his hand for quiet, "Okay, everybody, just simmer down. Both sides are right. I know this because I am a Blue citizen married to a Red citizen. I'll give you an example. Before we were married, I got Julianne pregnant. It was my fault because I didn't protect us with birth control. I thought abortion was the route to go because we weren't married yet, but Julianne said, 'Absolutely not!' She said she would rather raise the baby as a single mom than take its life. I reluctantly agreed, and we got married and had Little Clark. I totally love that little fellow, and I am so glad that we did not abort him. So, my point is that Blue and Red can work together...if they really try. Plus, if the Blue Nation goes broke, who's going to pay their infrastructure and military fees? If we Blues fail, the Reds will be left holding the debt bag. I suggest that Maria, Charles, and Leon get together and come up with a proposal to reunite the States."

"I'm always willing to talk, but I can guarantee that the Red Nation people will want nothing to do with a proposal to reunite the two nations back into one country. We Reds like what we have and have no intention of going backward!" said Charles.

"Okay, just begin to talk about possible reunification," said Seth. The three nodded in agreement as Seth continued, "Actually, we have a more pressing problem now. The people that refused to join either nation and fled to the various mountain areas have linked up via the internet and want to create their own nation too. The movement is led by Ethan James, a survivalist and former Hell's Angel biker. They are about 40,000 strong and heavily armed."

"Wow, 40,000! I knew those folks were out there but didn't realize there were so many. How do they live without being a citizen of a nation?" queried Clark.

"They live in a 'cash and barter culture' like many of the undocumented immigrants did before the time of the Great Consolidation in 2029. Some of them live off the land, while others are paid 'under the table' by the businesses they work for. They have begun to raid small community stores to steal supplies. They are well organized and have baffled small-town police and sheriff's departments. I believe it is time to talk to Ethan James and see if we can bring them into one of the new nations. I'd like to set up a meeting with James and our executive staff," replied Seth.

"Okay, Seth. Set it up. I look forward to meeting Mr. James and his crowd," said Clark with a broad smile.

*****

Ethan James and twenty other bikers came roaring into the small town of Bemidji, Minnesota, and headed for the armory on the north side of town, where they would meet with Clark, Seth, Nancy, their staff, and security personnel. The Red Blue Management Team of thirty-five people had spent the night in Minneapolis and then took jet-copters to the small regional airport for the 10 a.m. meeting at the local armory. The city officials of Bemidji had worked with the RBMT's transitional service unit to turn the abandoned armory into a pleasant place for the meeting. Supplemental heating, meeting rooms, restrooms, and a cafeteria were added to serve the participants.

Ethan Walter James was an average-sized man in his mid-fifties. Ethan had grown up fishing the lakes and hunting the woods of Northern Minnesota. Ethan finished high school in Bemidji and attended two years of college before dropping out to log the North woods. Ethan was rough-looking with his long hair and full beard, but he was intelligent and quite articulate for a lumberman. Ethan had actually amassed a small fortune with his logging efforts and was quietly settled in a rustic log cabin with his Native American wife, Lilly Red Hawk. Ethan and Lilly had one child, a daughter, who was a corporate attorney in the Twin Cities. When the United States was abandoned in favor of the Red and Blue Nations, Ethan and Lilly immediately headed for their survival cabin in the North woods. Ethan was politically aligned with Red philosophies but hated the idea of being forced to make the choice of choosing a new nation. Over the two and a half years that the new nations had existed, Ethan and Lilly had rallied support over the internet and short-wave radio for the idea of a third nation. The couple published a blog called "The Misfit Nation" that was read by over 40,000 adherents. Now it was time to act.

Ethan, Lilly, and their personal security guard, Garrett Stoner, walked into the meeting with the Red Blue Team after turning their weapons in at the metal detector. Ethan only carried a highway patrolman model Smith and Wesson .357 Magnum revolver, while Lilly surrendered her sawed-off double-barrel Remington Shotgun that she kept hidden under her large fur coat. She politely asked the security team to take good care of her weapon as it was her granddaddy's. Garrett, or The Beef, as most friends called him, turned in an eight-inch bowie knife and an Uzi that actually looked small in his huge hands. The three "Misfits" were ushered into a tile-floored room with redwood siding. The room held a single long table with eight boardroom-style rolling leather chairs. Clark, Seth, and Nancy rose immediately when the trio entered. Clark introduced himself, Seth, and Nancy as the heads of the Red Blue Team. Ethan James then introduced his wife, Lilly Red Hawk James, and their bodyguard Garrett Stoner.

As the six shook hands and greeted each other personally, Nancy gasped, "Beef, is that you?"

Garrett Stoner immediately saluted Admiral Nancy Choi and said as his voice cracked, "Yes, ma'am, Admiral...it's me." Nancy Choi grabbed the six-feet-five-inches 260-pound former Navy SEAL and buried her face in his burly chest as Beef broke down and cried like a little boy that had just been reunited with his mother.

After the embrace was broken, Nancy announced to the other five, "This man was my number one go-to guy when we were in the field. We served together on over twelve missions. He saved my life more than once, and I actually helped him out a time or two. I trusted this man with my life and still would today. Clark and Seth, if Garrett Stoner believes in the Misfit cause, then we need to earnestly listen to them."

"Well, by all means, Nancy," said Clark.

Seth motioned for everyone to take a seat as the attendants served water, hot tea, and coffee.

Clark began by saying, "I'm so glad you contacted us. We want to hear from you. Please tell us your story."

Ethan James began, "I never served in the military or was involved in civic affairs, but I've always been a proud American. I love the country that you dissolved. I understand why you did what you did, but I don't like being forced to choose between only two ways of living. There are a lot of ways to live. As you know, my wife Lilly is a Native American. Native American lands were stolen by the U. S. government, and the Native Americans were herded onto reservations, where many live today. I feel like our country was stolen from us by you all."

Clark interrupted, "Now, wait a minute. We didn't steal anything; we empowered the people—"

"Come on, Clark, don't get defensive. Let the man finish," said Seth.

"You're right, you're right. I apologize, Mr. James. Please go on," said Clark sheepishly.

Ethan continued, "I speak for liberals who believe the government should only be funded by the rich and for the conservatives to the right of Charles Sikes. We don't agree with each other, but one thing we do agree on is the right to make our own choices. We actually don't want a 'Misfit Nation'...we just want what the original Founding Fathers wanted, a land where everyone can pursue life, liberty, and happiness. With your tattoos and your computerized networks, your two nations have divided what used to be the American people in a way that Washington's governmental gridlock and political wrangling never did. Have you seen the 'Blue Ghetto' in New Orleans? People are dying there from drugs and disease, and the Blue Nation has no resources to help them. The Red Nation doesn't even care. They just let them die and look the other way until it's time to buy up more Blue property. Something has to change!"

The room sat in silence for a few moments, and then Seth spoke, "Ethan, Lilly, and Garrett, thank you for coming. We needed to hear from you. We have been so busy managing the day-to-day support operation of the two nations and our own family problems that we have neglected to see the hurting people all around us."

Clark added, "Thank you for opening our eyes to see the bigger picture. We will want to meet with you again…soon."

Nancy said, "I would like to request a specific list of changes to implement in our new nations that will allow each group to become stronger."

"We can certainly do that, Admiral Choi," stated Ethan.

The six continued to talk and swap ideas for another hour, and then lunch was served for all of the Misfit bikers and RBMT staff. The bikers roared off about 3 p.m. as Clark, Nancy, and Seth remained to discuss the meeting. Clark was convinced he could see even more need for re-unification after talking with the Misfits. However, he would have to put those revelations aside in the near future. Unbelievable disaster was on its way to the two nations.

CHAPTER 12

The Shaking

When Seth returned from the meeting with the Misfits, Julianne met him at their back door with a soft kiss and a glass of his favorite wine. Seth was extremely tired, as it was almost 10 p.m. He really wanted a hot shower and a good night's sleep, but he could tell that Julianne was anxious to talk about something. Seth sat on the couch next to his wife, and after a few minutes of small talk about Little Clark, Seth said, "Okay, beautiful, I can tell that you have something on your mind. Do you want to share it with me?"

"I know you are tired, babe, but this is really important," said Julianne with a somber look.

"Okay, sweetheart, I'm all ears. What' up?" asked Seth.

"Have you ever heard about the 1811 earthquakes along the New Madrid fault lines?" asked Julianne.

"Uh...no, I don't believe I have," said Seth while wearing a puzzled expression.

"Well," continued Julianne, "it was one of the worst natural disasters that this land ever experienced. Most people remember the San Francisco earthquake of 1906 because so much of the city was destroyed, and many lives were lost, but the 1811 quake would have been much worse if it had struck a populated area. In 1811, much of the area that we know as Arkansas, Missouri, and Tennessee was considered 'out west' and sparsely populated. The New Madrid quakes of 1811 were actually several times more powerful than the quake that destroyed San Francisco in 1906. This quake was so powerful that the Mississippi River actually ran backward for a period of time. Church bells were rung on the East coast, and windows were shaken in Washington, D. C."

"This is an amazing history lesson Julianne but why are you giving me this information now?" asked Seth.

Julianne took a deep breath and looked Seth directly in the eyes, and then said, "I talked with the Geological Service director today, and their agency is predicting a major quake in that area in the near future. If their predictions are true, Saint Louis, Memphis, and parts of Arkansas could be uninhabitable after a quake of the 1811 magnitude."

While Julianne and Seth were talking, the wild and domestic animals around the Saint Louis area were exhibiting strange behavior. Domestic dogs and cats were howling and screeching incessantly, while wild deer, turkeys, and raccoons were wandering into the back-yards of urban dwellers. Slight tremors could be felt within a hundred-mile radius of the Saint Louis area.

Seth gave the head of the Geological Service director, Eva Jenkins, a call the next morning and set up an emergency face-to-face meeting with himself, Clark, Julianne, Nancy, and the two prime ministers for the next afternoon. The team members that were not already in Dallas jet-coptered in for the 4 p.m. meeting.

Dr. Eva Jenkins was a short, stout fifty-five-year-old woman of African heritage. She had been the head of the U. S. Geological Agency before the Red and Blue Nations were formed and had assumed command of the privatized Geological Service that served both new nations. Dr. Jenkins had received her bachelor's degree in geological engineering from MIT and her PhD in geosciences from USC. Dr. Jenkins was a world-renowned expert in predicting seismic events.

Clark opened the meeting by welcoming everyone and then said, "I know this is not our usual protocol, but I believe that we should open this most important meeting with prayer. I hope I do not offend any here that are not people of faith, but I believe this is right for this time." He prayed, "Father, we ask You to give us wisdom as we consider what to do in this situation. We further ask You to prepare the nations for whatever the future holds. Thank You, Father...in Jesus' name, we pray.

Amen." Clark then addressed the team, "Now then, let's get to our purpose at hand. You have all met Dr. Jenkins...uh, Dr. Jenkins, would you please tell us what is on your mind?"

"Thanks for the introduction, Clark, and please, you may call me Eva." As Eva began to talk, a full-color holographic image of the New Madrid fault area sprang up in the middle of the round table where the group was seated. "You can see the fault line and projected area of possible damage to the land masses that were affected in the 1811 event. As you know, the area was largely un-populated then, and loss of life was minimal. However, a seismic event in the 8.9 range, like our projections, would involve many millions of people in the Missouri, Arkansas, and Tennessee areas. The results would be catastrophic."

Charles Sikes, the Red prime minister, interrupted, "But haven't the structures in those areas been prepared for a seismic event?"

"The structures in that area have what I would call modest anti-quake measures," continued Dr. Jenkins. "We must remember that the event that my Geological Service is predicting could be even larger than the 1811 series of quakes. The seismic scale is an exponential scale. An 8.9 event releases 31.7 times more energy than a 7.9 event like the one that destroyed 80 percent of San Francisco in 1906. Plus, the 1811 New Madrid event affected over eight times the area of the San Francisco quake. We could be in for a catastrophe greater than anything this land has ever seen."

The RBMT members were stunned. There was an incredible amount of brain power, political expertise, and military might represented at the table, but the general feeling was one of helplessness and impending doom.

"Is there anything we can do?" asked Julianne meekly.

"The first thing I would suggest is that we all do what Clark did to open this meeting. We should all pray as we have never prayed before. We will need God's help if we are to survive what I think is coming. The second thing I would suggest is that we get prepared to deal with a mega-disaster. Both nations will need to work together with the military and all of the privatized agencies that replaced FEMA, HUD, etc. We will need blood banks, search and rescue crews, and protection from looting when this thing hits," said Leon Brown.

"Eva, what's your best guess on when these events could take place?" asked Seth.

"That's hard to say, Seth, but we do know that the frequencies and strength of smaller seismic events are increasing. Over 200 micro-quakes occur every year in the NMSZ (New Madrid Seismic Zone) that stretches northeastwardly in a zig-zag fashion from Marked Tree, Arkansas, through Missouri, Tennessee, Kentucky, and to Cairo, Illinois. The whole fault line is about 125 miles long. One of the problems in predicting quakes in the NMSZ is that the fault lines are actually buried under 200 feet of soil. The Cascadia subduction zone that runs to the west of Portland and Seattle can actually be seen below the ocean waters offshore. The movement of that fault is much easier to record, whereas evidence of NMSZ activity disappears rather quickly in the soft soil. However, here's the scary part, although the number of micro-quakes is increasing overall, there are some regions where they have stopped. This means that a 7-plus quake could occur in those areas in the short term because the pressure that is building up is not being released by the micro-quakes," said Eva.

Seth chuckled, "You still didn't answer my question, Eva! What's your best guess on when a big quake could occur?"

Eva smiled, "Yeah, we scientific types don't like to be tied down. I would say from our data that a series of large quakes could occur within two months to two years, but my best guess would be three or four months."

"Wow, that's really quick. How can we prepare for something that is coming, but we don't know where or when?" asked Clark.

"And who's gonna pay for it? Not the BBN, you know the Broke Blue Nation!" said Charles in a huff.

Maria shot Charles a nasty look and replied, "We will do our part, Mr. Red Prime Minister!"

"Okay, you two, stop it! The rest of us are tired of your squabbling. We are looking at the possibility of a great disaster, and you two are acting like school children!" said Clark with a bright red face. "Now, I'm asking Leon, Nancy, Eva, Maria, and Charles to come up with a broad overview plan on how to prepare for this situation. Leon, will you chair this effort? You can present your ideas to the whole team and senior staff at 9 a.m., two days from now. Can you make that happen?" asked Clark.

"Yes, we can, Clark," said Leon as the others nodded their heads in agreement.

"Actually," said Eva. "Let me take this committee, with whatever staff they need, to our Geological Service headquarters outside of Saint Louis. We can tour the NMSZ and get a look at the freshest data that predicts the event. We can get back to you with our best plan of action in about four or five days."

"That's a better idea," said Clark. "We'll meet back in Dallas next Tuesday at 10 a.m. if y'all don't mind working the weekend. The jet-copters are waiting."

The team arrived at Scott Air Force Base in Illinois at 10 a.m. the next morning. A few of the adjunct scientific staff members would be coming in later, but the main committee members, composed of Nancy, Leon, Charles, Maria, and Eva, along with their security and staff members, all landed in sequence. Kirk and Sonya accompanied Admiral Nancy Choi as both attachés and security guards. The team was carried by Air Force personnel straight to the Geological Service headquarters, which was located about halfway between the air base and the city of Saint Louis. Eva had arranged for her senior scientist, Dr. Samuel M. Hocutt, to give the team a breakdown of what was going on geologically in the fault area.

The team was invited into a large conference room where Dr. Hocutt offered them refreshments while his aides prepared the final touches to his presentation. Everybody settled into their seats while Dr. Hocutt began his address, "I wanted to thank all of you for coming to this research center. We live with this stuff every day, but I believe it will help our cause to get a fresh set of eyes on our data as we prepare a plan to help this area survive. So, let's get started."

The huge holovision whirred to life and showed 3D pictures of devastation from the earthquakes of the NMSZ that occurred in 1811 and 1812. Dr. Hocutt explained, "Actually, there were major quakes during a three-month period, and over 2,000 aftershocks followed. You all know the story of the Mississippi River running backward, and that is true; however, that is more of a phenomenon than a seriously damaging effect of that series of quakes. As you can see from the pictures, the real damage was caused by the thirty-foot drops in ground level and the huge sand blow results that are still visible over a hundred years later. Could you imagine a sand blow happening in the middle of a school yard or a thirty-foot sinkhole opening up under a skyscraper? The results would be devastating."

"Okay, Dr. Hocutt, I know what a sinkhole is, but what in the world is a sand blow?" interrupted Charles.

"Oh, sorry, I should have explained that terminology. A sand blow is like a waterspout, except it's on land. As pressure is released below, the sand literally blows up in a spout. As the sand blows up, the ground beneath it sinks down." Hocutt continued, "So, what can we do? I believe we should begin a campaign to educate the populace around the fault area concerning the reality of this threat. We can encourage every household and business to stock up on water, food, and electric generators. The Emergency Management Agency has a good supply of those items that have been purchased from the fees paid by the Red and Blue Nations. The EMA funds and equipment could be used to store emergency supplies at schools and other public buildings."

"But aren't you worried about panic and overreaction from the populace?" asked Nancy.

"Not really," said Dr. Hocutt. "We are still waiting on a major event in the San Andreas fault area, but the people of California keep on building and living as though nothing will ever happen. California has strengthened its building codes and has a readiness agency, but it's hard to get excited about a disaster that has been delayed for well over a hundred years. What we must do in the NMSZ area is create a limited amount of panic. I want to see the entire populace making survival preparations. I would ask Admiral Choi to station troops with rescue and medical training along the most populated area of the 125-mile fault line. Also, I have already asked the governors of the affected states to contact the Red Cross about having a significant amount of blood transferred to areas just outside the fault area."

After a lunch break, the team continued to hear presentations regarding the chance of a big quake occurring in the near future. Roundtable discussions continued until 5 p.m., when the team and staff were carried back to the Ruby Crown Hotel close to downtown Saint Louis. The next two days were filled with conference calls to the governors of the states that could be affected and planning sessions between high-ranking military officers and disaster agency specialists. By Friday at noon, everybody was satisfied that the team had achieved a workable plan. The information would be released to the media on Monday so the NMSZ residents could begin to prepare for possible disasters. The team enjoyed an on-site catered lunch and then headed back to the Ruby Crown for a little downtime before they jet-coptered back to Dallas on Saturday morning.

"Hey, Stretch, I mean Admiral Choi," laughed Sonya, "Eva and I are going to copter up to Memphis to take in Graceland and hear a little country music afterward. My grandparents loved Elvis, and I really want to see his burial site and home. We would love for you to come with us."

"I appreciate the offer, ladies, but my physical fitness has really suffered this week. I plan to do some laps in the hotel pool. Kirk is going to hang around with me as my official bodyguard," said Nancy.

"Anyone else have plans?" queried Eva.

"Well, I've got a date on a Mississippi riverboat with two handsome gentlemen," said Maria as she rolled her big brown eyes. "That's right, Leon and Charles have booked a supper cruise for the three of us plus a few security agents on the Delta Steamer. It is a real steam-driven paddle boat, and I hear that the food is fabulous. We leave at 3 p.m. and steam south towards Cape Girardeau before reversing course back to Saint Louis. We should be back by 11 p.m."

Everyone went back to their hotel rooms before embarking on their "fun-night" exploits. Nancy headed to the hotel workout room with Kirk in tow while Eva and Sonya changed clothes for the copter ride to Memphis. Maria, Leon, and Charles took a taxi to the pier where the Delta Steamer was docked. It was going to be a special night for the hard-working group.

The Ruby Crown Hotel in Saint Louis was famous for its food, as well as its luxurious accommodations. Four five-star restaurants with international themes were located in the complex. Nancy had eaten the Italian, Southern American, and French cuisine on previous nights, but tonight she and her bodyguard/attaché Kirk dined at the Ruby Crown Dragon Hibachi Steakhouse. Nancy and Kirk had become extremely good friends since her decision for Christ. Nancy had become the older sister Kirk never had, while she looked upon him as her everyday pastor. Nancy texted spiritual questions to Kirk on a regular basis, and Kirk led a weekly Bible study at Nancy's apartment. Sonya and several other RBMT staff attended the Bible study and potluck dinner. As the couple looked over the menu, a slight shaking could be felt in the room. The waiter who was filling their water glasses chuckled and said, "Don't worry about that little shaking. We get 'em every few days... helps the chef toss the salad." Kirk laughed at what was probably an old joke, but Nancy just flashed a quick uneasy smile. After the fantastic dinner, Nancy and Kirk went back to their respective rooms to rest before meeting at the rooftop pool on the tenth floor.

Kirk met Nancy at her room door to escort her to the pool. Nancy was wearing a cover-up over her swimsuit and had braided her long dark hair into a single pigtail. Kirk took a seat in a poolside chair as Nancy dove into the pool and completed two lengths underwater before starting her freestyle swim. Nancy, the Navy SEAL, was like a fish in water and loved to swim laps for hours on end. Tonight, she would swim for about thirty minutes while Kirk busied himself by reading a book on the history of Saint Louis.

The 7.2 magnitude earthquake hit at 9:50 p.m. Kirk was ejected out of his chair into the guardrail as the building swayed to the north. His feet shattered a tempered glass panel between two of the metal posts of the guardrail that made up the decorative barrier surrounding the pool area.

As the shaking continued, Kirk could feel his lower body slipping over the building edge. As Kirk was frantically grabbing for the metal poles to keep from going over the side, the building reversed course and sent him sliding on his back across the buckling tile into the diving board support structure, which was thankfully anchored firmly into the concrete. Kirk grabbed onto the metal structure and watched in disbelief as Nancy, encapsulated by a bubble of water, was hurled out of the pool and passed right over his head. Nancy crashed onto the now-broken tile floor and slid into the side of the concrete pump house. Kirk managed to crawl the fifteen feet to Nancy and pulled the groaning and bleeding admiral by her feet over to the diving board support pipes, where they both held on tightly as the shaking continued.

*****

Sonya and Eva had become good friends over the short period of time they had known each other. With Sonya being born and raised in Louisiana and Eva having done her undergraduate work at Ole Miss, both women were totally familiar with the culture of the Deep South. They enjoyed the tour of Graceland and marveled at the gold records and green shag carpet hanging on the wall. Both women were reverently silent as they stood in the back garden and watched the flickering flame at Elvis' grave dance in the wind.

After the Graceland tour and a delicious meal of barbecued ribs accompanied by some good country music, Eva and Sonya headed to the Memphis Pyramid.

The Memphis Pyramid, or just The Pyramid as the locals call it, was built in the late 1980s as a 20,142-seat arena. The Pyramid is constructed of a steel frame wrapped with glazed bronze glass. The Pyramid was currently being used as a hotel, shopping mall, and multiple restaurant venues. The Pyramid is located on the banks of the Mississippi River and has become a majestic landmark for the area.

Eva and Sonya entered the Pyramid at about 8:20 p.m. that evening, and walked around the gigantic structure, window shopping and picking up a few souvenirs for their friends and family.

They stopped on the fourth floor to have an ice cream cone and sat down on a wrought iron bench next to the 1,200-gallon aquarium containing fish species from the Mississippi River. They watched the huge channel catfish move along the bottom while bass and bream navigated the upper waters in silent beauty.

Then the shaking began—a low rumble at first—followed by the sound of crashing glass and terrified screams. Eva and Sonya both were thrown off the bench onto the floor into a pool of water, aquarium gravel, and wriggling fish. A large channel catfish gashed Sonya's hand with its dorsal fin as it flopped about on the floor. The shaking lasted about fifteen seconds and then abruptly stopped. The two women cautiously rose to their feet and looked at the devastation and terror around them. Moans could be heard coming from all directions, and the sounds of groaning steel and shattering glass permeated the air. Eva shrieked, "Come on, Sonya...follow me...there will be aftershocks! Run, now!" Sonya followed Eva past the elevator and into the stairwell. "Quick! Under the stair cavity!" shouted Eva. Just as the women crawled under the stair cavity, the shaking started again...this time more fiercely than before. The two friends grabbed each other tightly and tucked their heads into their chests. The sound of breaking glass and concrete grinding against steel was deafening.

Both women began to shout their prayers out loud, "Help us, Jesus! Protect us, O Lord! Please protect the people in this building and bring peace to the ground!" Eva and Sonya continued to pray until the shaking stopped. They cautiously crawled out from under the stairwell and began to walk down the stairs toward the ground floor. There was a good bit of rubble that they had to push aside, as well as a few twisted steel beams to navigate as they headed toward what they thought was an exit. They continued to hear screams and moans but kept going toward the ground floor.

"We've got to go back...and help those people! They... sound like they...are dying!" said Eva between sobs.

"I assure you that we will do all we can to help them," said Sonya, "but my job right now is to get you to safety before there is another aftershock. We can't lose you or your valuable expertise during this emergency. C'mon, Eva! Let's get out of this building and let the first responders do their jobs."

The women reached the bottom floor and were greeted by broken glass, steel beams in disarray, and injured people in the main lobby. Sonya took Dr. Jenkins away from the building and towards an open garden behind the complex. The only light was coming from the moon and the stars as the quake had left that part of the city without electrical power. Every step was treacherous as the two shaken women made their way across a once beautiful garden. Now, downed trees, twisted metal, and broken glass littered their path to safety. It was like being terrified and blind at the same moment.

Sonya and Eva sat on a steel park bench that was miraculously undamaged and said nothing for a few minutes. Finally, Eva spoke with warm tears trickling down her cheeks, "I can't believe I missed the signals so badly...I knew this was coming but thought we had a few months to prepare. People are dead, and it's my fault... Oh, God...how did I miss this?"

"Not one more word of that talk, Eva," said Sonya rather sharply. "You are not God...you're just one of His children who is trying to help. Earthquakes have been happening for millions of years, and the fact that you could predict it at all boggles my mind."

"I know you are right," said Eva quietly. "I just hate all this destruction. Say, how is your catfish gash?"

"Oh, it's not bad...probably won't need stitches. He probably heard that I like to eat his cousins!" said Sonya with a chuckle. "Let me fire up my sat phone and see if we can contact the rest of the team."

*****

The Delta Steamer was about an hour from the port in Saint Louis when the quake rumbled into its location on the Mississippi River. Leon, Marie, and Charles, surrounded by a five-person deployment of the RBMT guard team, were in a private dining area on the deck of the Delta Steamer. This particular guard deployment was captained by Taylor Wallace. Taylor was a retired

Marine officer and, at fifty years old, was still as tough as nails. He considered it a great honor to guard both prime ministers and Leon.

When the underground plates shifted, a wave much like a tsunami flipped the Delta Steamer up at a thirty-degree angle and then pushed it toward the eastern bank. Taylor, who was closest to Maria, covered her with his large body as she came sliding by his position. The two bumped into the guardrail. As the boat began its descent back toward the river, Taylor, along with several others, flew over the guardrail into the turbulent Mississippi River. Maria's legs had been jammed around a rail post that kept her from flying into the inky, cold waters with the others while the Delta Steamer crashed back down into the river. Even though the riverboat journey was now extremely rough, people began to crawl about on the slippery, water-soaked, and debris-filled deck. Maria sat up and peered into the darkness looking for Taylor Wallace. He was nowhere to be seen. Maria heard the moans and screams from the passengers and realized that a low moaning was coming from her own mouth. The night was pitch black, except for a few battery-operated emergency lights that shined eerily over the passengers moving slowly around the deck. Maria "duck-walked" over broken glass and pieces of the ceiling until she got back to their table, which was bolted to the floor and still intact. She found Leon holding onto a table leg. Blood was oozing from a gash in his head, and his left wrist was twisted into a strange shape.

Two of the guards near the table were beginning to regain their balance, but Charles was nowhere in sight.

The pain in Leon's left wrist was unbearable. *Did it hurt Mark this much when he was thrown from his bike and landed on his little ten-year-old wrist?* Leon's first born, Mark, had been found crumpled in a pile after the accident by the next-door neighbor. The good Samaritan had scooped Mark up into his arms and carried him to Leon. Betty, Leon's wife and Mark's mom, had almost fainted when she saw the blood, dirt, and fear covering her son. Mark wasn't crying anymore but repeatedly said, "It hurts. It hurts, Daddy. It hurts, Mommy!" Leon knew what that meant now. Drifting in and out of consciousness, Leon could see the faces of his loved ones. He wondered if they were all right. He mumbled their names, "Betty, Mark, Ella, Claire, Annagale...where are you?" The guards, who doubled as first responders, gained their wits about them and immediately began to triage Leon.

The bump on his head had caused confusion and shock, as well as a deep cut running the length of his left profile. The guard with the medic backpack fumbled inside for antiseptic, butterfly Band-Aids, and a temporary splint for Leon's broken wrist. It would have to do for now. By elevating his legs and covering his wet body with a blanket, they hoped to break the shock that was creeping over Leon's being.

Maria could faintly hear Charles moaning and calling her name. It was hard to tell exactly where he was due to the screams, moans, and shouts around her. She was finally able to make out his crushed form under a barstool where he lay against the bar wall. Walking was now possible, so Maria and one of the least injured guards walked the twenty feet to Charles. Charles was shaking and calling Maria's name as he lay in a growing pool of blood. Even in the dim light, Maria could see that Charles was not under the barstool but that one of the stool legs had actually pierced his chest cavity and left a gaping hole that was the source of the blood. Maria had worked as a registered nurse in an ER before she went back to school and got involved in politics, and she knew that they had to stop the bleeding fast or Charles would die. Evidently, the guard had some medical training, too, as he immediately began to put pressure on the wound. Maria noticed one of the crew members had lit a flare to signal their position to any help that might be available. Maria shouted to the crew member, "Hey, give me one of your flares!" The crew member ignored her, so Maria ran to him and said, "I said give me one of your flares! The prime minister is dying! I can cauterize his wound with a flare. Give it to me now!" The dazed crew member handed Maria a flare and went back to methodically waving his flare back and forth. Maria raced back over to Charles and the guard and lit the flare. Maria instructed the guard to quickly pull the barstool leg out of Charles' chest, and she then shoved the flare deeply into Charles' open wound. Charles screamed in pain and tried to move as the security guard held him down. Maria quickly pulled the flare out as the pungent smell of chemical fumes and burning flesh filled the air. After about three seconds of burning, the flare had cauterized the wound, and the bleeding stopped. Charles whimpered softly before passing out. Maria sat back on the rocking deck and began to sob violently.

*****

Nancy and Kirk stood up slowly and assessed their situation—no broken bones but plenty of scrapes and bruises. "Okay, Kirk, we're basically in one piece, so let's get down to the ground floor before the aftershocks take us out," said Nancy calmly. Kirk activated the flashlight on his phone and started toward the stairwell from the roof. The stairwell door was jammed closed, so Kirk took a long piece of metal debris and pried the door open enough for the two of them to slip through. They began to work their way down the ten floors with only the light from Kirk's phone. "I hope you charged that thing up," said Nancy.

"I'm at about 70 percent. We should be fine," mumbled Kirk. The stairs were separated by a four-foot gap on the eighth floor, so the pair went back up to floor nine and found the central staircase to continue their descent. Most hotel residents were using that main stairway to get down to the ground. There were a few minor injuries, but the majority of the residents were in fairly good shape. Fortunately, the Ruby Crown complex had been built to survive a major quake.

*****

The news services began carrying the "Great Central Quake" story almost immediately. The Geological Service headquarters had survived the event with little damage, so Dr. Hocutt was available for consultation with the news services. Dr. Hocutt shared the following statement with the nation: "A series of earthquakes don't usually hit across the fault line at the same time. An epicenter of the quake is the point where the quake is the strongest, but additional quakes and aftershocks can run the fault line in different time frames. The epicenter for this seismic event was midway between the rural village of Whitewater, Missouri, and the Mississippi River. The epicenter measured 7.6 on the Richter scale. Fortunately, the area is not highly populated, but the additional quakes in the Saint Louis and Memphis area were substantial enough to do significant damage to those large cities. Since the quakes were at night, students were out of class and unaffected, and most large buildings had been vacated for the evening. Now, it's a matter of search and rescue, clean up, and rebuild."

Clark, Seth, and Julianne were immediately notified when the quakes struck. Nancy and Kirk were the first ones to contact Clark by sat phone. Their lack of serious injuries was a relief. Sonya also called in and let the Dallas team know that she and Eva were merely bruised and scratched from their experience at the Pyramid. However, nobody had heard from Maria, Charles, and Leon. About an hour later, Maria called in and related the amazing details of the Delta Steamer being slammed around by the river tsunami. After Maria had saved Charles' life by cauterizing his chest wound with the flare, an onboard doctor had made a makeshift neck brace to stabilize Charles' head before he and Leon were loaded onto the first rescue craft that had come alongside the Delta Steamer. Other rescue boats with search lights were busy looking for survivors that had been thrown overboard. Taylor Wallace had been holding onto a large portion of the Delta Steamer's siding and was rescued from the murky waters about an hour after the search began. All team members and the security detail had survived the most horrendous dinner cruise of all time.

Clark and Seth went on holovision at 9 a.m. the next morning and assured the two nations that military and joint service agencies would assist the affected cities in search and rescue, clean-up, and rebuilding. Admiral Choi was going to take the lead in deploying military assistance, while Leon used his formidable administrative skills to unite the service agencies in getting help directly to the damaged areas. Surprisingly, the citizens of the two nations were coming together to reach out to the devastated areas. Hope was in the air.

CHAPTER 13

The Healing Begins

The first order of business for the Red Blue Management Team was to see the earthquakes' actual devastation and fine-tune the rescue, clean-up, and rebuilding efforts. Since Charles was still in the hospital recovering from his wounds, Clark, Seth, Nancy, Leon, Maria, and Ethan James, the newest member of the team, inspected the affected areas. The team boarded an old-fashioned non-jet helicopter so they could see the damage in greater detail. The team made scheduled stops in Memphis, Missouri, and the outlying areas as they tried to fully understand the magnitude of the problem facing the two nations.

The devastation was unbelievable. Some buildings had tumbled to the ground, while others were in a partial state of collapse and posed an even greater danger. Whole neighborhoods had been swallowed by giant sinkholes, while other communities had been partially covered by dirt and rock from the sand blows. Highways were destroyed as giant shards of rock rose to pierce the asphalt.

Since Interstates and some overpasses serving I-24 and I-55 were flattened, supply and rescue vehicles were using two-lane roads and "pig paths" to get basic supplies to the survivors.

Marine transport helicopters were being used to supply essential necessities to the populace and airlift the seriously wounded to hospitals outside the quake zone.

The team visited Carbondale, Missouri, and heard the mayor recall how their house had dropped partially into a sinkhole during the quake. The mayor, Andy Fuller, and his wife, Karen, were watching holovision when the quake hit. The house lurched over at a forty-degree angle as it slid into the blackness of the hole. Andy and Karen were dumped out of their recliners and slid from the den to the dining room, where they were stopped by the large dining room chairs. The cabinetry full of antique china and silverware crashed across the dining room table, scattering the family heirlooms across the area. Karen sustained minor cuts from the falling glass, while the mayor only suffered minor bruising. Andy and Karen crawled uphill and out of the front door, where they stood trembling in what was left of their front yard and tearfully thanked God that they were alive. At first light, Mayor Fuller, Police Chief John Shirley, and Fire Chief Tim Martin formed a coalition that restored some semblance of order and saved many of the town's residents. Hands with red tattoos and hands with blue tattoos worked alongside each other with no regard to national affiliation. There was no political or ideological talk at all, as neighbors helped neighbors to survive. There was some minor looting, but that was unnecessary as the local stores unlocked their doors and invited the people in to take what they needed.

As the team listened to the leaders and townspeople of Carbondale, Clark instructed the cameramen traveling with them to record the people of Carbondale working together. The residents of nursing homes and ambulatory hospital patients were being cared for in the undamaged portions of their facilities or in tents procured from the National Guard Armory. The people of Carbondale were serving each other with true love and compassion, and Clark had it recorded to use as a teaching tool for the rest of the two nations.

Clark's broadcast of the unity in Carbondale produced a flood of people from every corner of former America. Food, clothing, and other essentials were brought to the stricken areas in pick-up trucks, vans, and sedans. The spirit of unity was also being expressed in house-to-house prayer meetings in most neighborhoods. The churches were full as the message of unity in Christ was preached. Mosques and synagogues were also reaching out to the earthquake victims.

The Misfits sent over 10,000 construction and timber workers down from Minnesota into the most severely damaged areas. They brought backhoes, front-end loaders, and other heavy equipment to help the people rebuild and recover. The Misfits had worked the land for their necessities during the last three years of change and were willing to share their expertise with anyone who would listen.

After three months of rebuilding was underway in Carbondale, the Red Blue Management Team, along with the Misfits' leadership, were invited to a Celebration of Rebuilding in Unity. The celebration was complete with speeches on the repaired courthouse steps and a parade that featured the local school bands marching with numerous pieces of construction equipment. The mayor rode proudly atop a backhoe that he had learned to operate during the crisis.

The whole town was invited to a Victory in Unity picnic at the large staging area for the rescue, recovery, and rebuilding efforts. About 2,000 people had shown up to share a meal of barbeque with all the trimmings. Security was tight because the whole RBMT was in attendance.

The major news outlets were filming and broadcasting the event live. After Clark said a blessing over the food, the mayor announced that dinner was served, and the hungry folks began the feast. Nancy was seated at a table beside one of the ponds that dotted the landscape. Kirk, her bodyguard, sat across from her, and Garrett Stoner, aka Beef, her unofficial bodyguard, was seated next to her right side while they laughed, joked, and enjoyed the food.

The aftershock hit without warning. There had been sporadic mild aftershocks during the three-month period, but this one would probably have registered a 5.5 on the Richter scale. The tables shook violently, and the picnickers fell helplessly to the ground as the tremors rumbled through the area. Several small sinkholes opened up, and tables, chairs, and people fell two or three feet to the bottom of the sinkhole. The sinkhole that opened up under Nancy's table caused the pond to splash into the open earth. As Nancy fell backward toward the shallow mud hole that had been formed by the tremor, she felt Beef's two strong arms grab her by the waist and sling her towards Kirk. Kirk grabbed her by the wrist and pulled her to safe ground as the chairs on Nancy's corner of the table and Beef tumbled into the muddy hole.

When the rumbling stopped, Kirk and Nancy both headed straight for the watery sinkhole that had engulfed Beef. They expected to see Beef smiling as he climbed out of the muddy pit, but what they saw both shocked and terrified them. Beef was writhing in pain in the shallow water as eight to ten water moccasins struck him repeatedly. When the water had emptied into the hole, a nest of water moccasins poured in with the marshy pond water.

The water moccasin is North America's only poisonous water snake. The water moccasin is also called a cotton mouth because of the white lining of the inside of its mouth. The bite of the moccasin is extremely painful as the snake injects a toxin that causes hemorrhaging at the site of the bite. However, few people die from the bite of the water moccasin if they are treated with antivenom. Left untreated, a single bite can cause death in two hours to two days. Water moccasins have a reputation for being aggressive, but actually, they will run from a fight unless threatened. In Beef's case, the aftershock had disrupted the nest of breeding snakes and toppled it out of the aquatic reeds and into the opening sinkhole. They attacked their supposed aggressor with slithering fury.

Kirk was able to grab one of Beef's ankles and began to drag the screaming man out of the pit. Nancy and a couple of the security guards helped Kirk pull the 260-pound man out of the pit and onto dry land. A couple of the moccasins were still attached to Beef's body. Nancy quickly grabbed each snake just behind the head, pulled the creatures off, and flung them back into the water. Two doctors were in attendance, and they quick-ly came to the stricken man's aid, but there was nothing they could do. The amount of poison that had been in-jected into Beef's body made it impossible to save him, even with anti-venom. Beef's screaming had turned to a gentle moan as he lay motionless on the ground while a sobbing Nancy kneeled beside him and held his snake-bitten hand. He mouthed "I love you" just before his eyes glazed over, and his breathing ceased.

Garrett "Beef" Stoner had given his life to save the woman he loved.

CHAPTER 14

The Funeral

Beef had become a national icon. The image of him on a backhoe as he cleared rubble from the quake-torn areas was used as a symbol of unity between the two nations. News agencies often carried coverage of the huge man as he selflessly worked to rebuild the devastated areas.

Beef had been interviewed more than once on national holovision, so his quick smile, good looks, and hearty laugh were known all over the land. Many of both the Red and Blue children had begun to grow their hair out and wear it in a ponytail just like Beef. A major toy maker was to come out with a Beef action figure just in time for Christmas. The action figure would be wearing Beef's camouflage shirt and blue jeans and sporting a red ball cap with a blue bill. For a few more dollars, a toy backhoe similar to the one Beef always operated could be purchased with the action figure. The toy manufacturer ramped up production after hearing of Beef's death.

Beef's funeral was covered by all the major news outlets. All of the Red Blue Management Team members
were present, and Clark was picked by Beef's mom to
do the eulogy. The plain oak casket was draped in the
flags of both nations and sat outside on a simple wood-
en platform located in Oak River Park outside Bemidji,
Minnesota, Beef's hometown. The Park was just big
enough to accommodate about 4,000 mourners plus
the myriad of cables and cameras required to holocast
the funeral live.

Clark began the service with an opening prayer, and
then the sounds of "Free Bird" by Lynyrd Skynyrd filled
the airways. Beef didn't care much for the music of the
current day but had fallen in love with music from the
'60s and '70s when he was a boy. Just as the song was
ending, about fifty of Beef's closest Misfit buddies came
roaring in on their Harleys. Three times they circled the
platform that was holding the casket and then roared
off toward the back of the park, where they stationed
themselves on each side of the road leading back out
to the highway. Those on the left side of the road held
a Blue Nation flag, while those on the right held a Red
Nation flag.

Clark began in his best preacher's voice, "Garrett
Ridgeway Stoner, or Beef as his friends called him, was
a great but unusual man. He served the former United
States of America as a Navy SEAL and distinguished

himself on the battlefield in the Jihadist War. Beef attained the rank of chief petty officer and received the Silver Star, Bronze Star, and two Purple Hearts for his military actions...."

Clark's words faded from Nancy's mind as she thought back to the first time she had seen Garrett Stoner. Nancy had been deployed as a lieutenant commander over SEAL Team Three in Southern Syria. Even though she had operational command, Nancy wanted to be close to the individual men and women that made up the six platoons. Nancy had called for a meeting with all six platoons in the mess tent outside the infirmary in the west staging area. Nancy had always been in the habit of arriving early for any meetings she was involved in and was striding toward the meeting place when she was stopped in her tracks.

The men's shower facility was composed of an open-air area covered by opaque plastic that contained four shower stations, and the dusty ground had been overlaid with pallets obtained from the munitions corp. Normally the plastic covering went up about ten feet, where it was attached to multiple poles forming the perimeter of the shower. About twenty men were laughing and talking as they showered in advance of the meeting. As Nancy walked by, she noticed that in one corner of the shower area, plastic sheeting had been ripped halfway down from the pole and exposed about four feet of the shower bullpen. As Nancy had stopped to make a repair note on her hand-held device, she felt a pair of eyes looking at her. She looked up to see a huge SEAL staring at her. He was only visible from the waist up but was truly an amazing specimen of a man. His huge frame looked like it had been chiseled from tan granite. He was all of six feet five with a forty-eight-inch chest that tapered down to a slim thirty-six-inch waist. His arms and shoulders looked like the product of many hours in the weight room. His hair was cut close on the sides but full of matted blonde locks on top. Steam from the showers silhouetted his frame while water dripped over his rugged chin. Nancy tried to keep walking but couldn't; she was frozen in her tracks.

Suddenly the huge man smiled, saluted, and then bellowed out, "Chief Petty Officer Stoner, at your command, ma'am!" Nancy silently saluted, turned swiftly, and walked toward the meeting tent. Nancy was a woman in command of the most elite fighting force in the world and had seen many fit SEALs, but this one unnerved her. It had to be that smile.

Nancy snapped back to the present as Clark droned on. Suddenly Clark said, "Now, I'd like to call on Admiral Choi to speak of her remembrance of Garrett Stoner." Nancy rose slowly and made the short walk to the platform and the microphone. Nancy was an accomplished speaker, but this was going to be difficult.

Just before Nancy began, she saw Sonya wink at her from the front row and mouth the words, "You can do this, Stretch."

Nancy began, "Garrett Stoner and I were deployed with SEAL Team Three in Southern Syria during the Jihad Wars. I was his commander, and he was my chief. Garrett was an excellent SEAL. He was brave, he was caring, and he followed orders to a T, but he also made us all laugh. Garrett's unselfish actions are also why I am standing here today."

Nancy cleared her throat and continued, "We were scheduled to meet the local leaders of the Free Syria movement at 2 p.m. on a Friday afternoon. The meeting place was an annex building that had supposedly been cleared of any Jihadist sympathizers. Garret was by my side, and six other heavily armed SEALs were with me. As I was shaking hands with the leaders, one of their Syrian guards pulled out a small firearm and pointed it directly at my chest. It all happened so fast that I couldn't move. I was in the middle of a handshake, and then I was facing death. The shot toward me and Beef's movement were simultaneous. Beef lurched in front of me and took the bullet in his upper chest just above his body armor. Two of the other SEALs killed the gunman instantly as the other four covered the remaining guards with their weapons. We later found out that the gunman had acted alone."

Nancy paused to wipe away a tear and then continued in a shaky voice, "Beef Stoner not only saved my life but preserved the integrity of our talks with the local leaders. There was a corpsman in the vicinity that quickly attended to Beef's wounds. The bullet had broken his collar bone and pierced the underlying subclavian vein. Thank God it wasn't an artery. It took about ten weeks for Beef to completely heal up, but he refused to call it quits and returned to active duty. He continued to serve me and our platoon until the end of the war. I hugged him goodbye just before he left for Minnesota, and I went to my next assignment at the Pentagon. Garrett Stoner was a patriot, a servant, and a man that loved others in a selfless way. I will greatly miss him."

Nancy finished by thanking Beef's family and his Misfit friends. Sniffles were heard all through the crowd as the SEALs folded and handed an old American flag to Garrett's mother. After the 21-gun salute, Clark said a final prayer, and Beef's body was transferred to the local cemetery for internment next to his father.

After the funeral, Nancy, Sonya, and Kirk met for coffee at Mae's Diner on the outskirts of Bemidji. A couple of security guards were at another table between the threesome and the door.

Kirk spoke softly, "Nancy, I know Beef was the love of your life, but it was a love that was buried by time, duty, and distance. But there is something I want to share with you. You know...Beef and I had become fairly good friends. We loved to shoot pool or play cards together. About three weeks before his death, I felt compelled to share the gospel with him. Beef never went to church much and never really heard the gospel. When I told him about Jesus' love for him and how to be saved, he grabbed hold of salvation like a kid in a candy store. I gave him a Bible with his name on it, and he began reading it and praying with great zeal."

Suddenly Nancy began to sob and cry, "He was saved! He was saved! I'll see him again in heaven...Oh, thank you, Kirk...thank you so much..." Then Nancy and Sonya held each other and cried while Kirk smiled and whispered, "Thank You, Father!"

CHAPTER 15

The Misfit Revolt

Ethan James had been drinking in the Red Cat Bar since 4 p.m. His wife, Lilly, had stayed in their hotel room after Ethan had said that he was going out for a drink, as she had no desire to be around her husband when he was drinking. His language, his manners, and most of his reasoning ability disappeared a little more with each shot of Jack Daniels Tennessee sipping whiskey.

Even though Ethan was born in Minneapolis, Minnesota, he related to Southern culture. He loved to fish and hunt and had a huge collection of weapons. He had built his own shooting range behind the cabin where he and Lilly lived. Ethan was proficient with semi-automatic rifles and pistols, but his favorite weapon was his blue-steel Smith and Wesson Model 28 357 Magnum revolver with a 6-inch barrel. This gun was produced in 1966 and was carried by Ethan's great uncle Charles James, a state trooper in East Alabama during the 1970s. The gun was given to Ethan's grandfather about 2010 and then passed on to Ethan's father, who had willed the pistol to Ethan.

Ethan didn't bother to carry a concealed weapon but wore the holstered 357 on his right hip. As Ethan got drunker, he began to rant against the Red and Blue Nations and the team that had created them. "These nations need to be disbanded and forgotten," shouted Ethan. "I believe those earthquakes were God's judgment on us for the creation of those fake nations!"

A few of the patrons mumbled in agreement, but most people just looked the other way. They had heard drunks ramble on about politics before. Finally, the bartender told Ethan to either shut up or leave. Ethan stumbled out to his Harley and fumbled around in the various pockets of his leather jacket, looking for his keys. Ethan was a proud man, and even though he knew he might be too inebriated to control his Harley on the winding, hilly roads of Tennessee, he would give it a try anyway.

"Hey patriot, can I give you a lift?" asked a husky female voice. "Actually, you left your key ring in your saddlebag, and I retrieved it so no one would steal that beautiful vintage Night Train motorcycle," the woman continued as she chuckled.

"Yeah, I could use a lift...I'm sure in no condition to drive," mumbled Ethan. He staggered to the woman's two-seater sports car and piled into the passenger's seat. "I'm in room 206 of that little motel on the corner of 5th and Main...or at least that's what I seem to remember..." said Ethan in a slurred voice.

They arrived at the motel in a few minutes, and the tall, muscular, slender woman helped Ethan out of the car and up to the second floor of the concrete structure. By this time, Ethan could barely put one foot in front of the other. The woman knocked on the door marked 206, and Lilly appeared with a frantic look on her face and said, "Oh, thank you so much! I was so worried...he wouldn't answer his cell."

The two women helped Ethan to the bed, where he promptly passed out, and Lilly beckoned for the woman to sit in one of the chairs opposite the little kitchenette. "Thank you again! I had no idea where he was. You are a godsend!" said Lilly with a look of relief. "Would you like a cup of coffee or perhaps a soda?"

"No, thank you, I'm in a rush." The woman handed Lilly Ethan's key ring and started for the door. "I'll drop by tomorrow morning, and we'll go get his Harley," said the woman in a husky voice.

"That would be wonderful! By the way, what is your name?" asked Lilly.

"My name is Angelica Jacquez, but most people call me Angel Jack."

Angel Jack figured Ethan had slept off his drunken stupor by 11 a.m., so she pulled up to the motel just in time to see Lilly going in the door with a couple of coffees. Angel Jack was wearing tight-fitting black jeans and a lightweight camo jacket. She wore biker shoes and a red-colored baseball cap with the word "Patriot" emblazoned on the front in blue and white letters. She carried a Barretta 9mm pistol inside the waist band of her jeans and her favorite pearl-handled stiletto in the right pocket of her jacket.

Lilly spotted Angel Jack as she exited her 2019 black Mercedes GT-class convertible and shouted for her to come on up to the room. Angel Jack patted the Mercedes as she rounded the front end and headed for room 206. She didn't love much in life, but Angel Jack cherished this automobile. She had tinkered with the fuel system and turbo package until she had raised the stock horsepower from 469 to 499. The car was over forty years old, a true classic, but the shiny black paint had very few nicks. The small trunk had been fitted with a rack system that held additional weapons—a Mossberg tactical shotgun, an MG 40 military assault rifle, an old-style Israeli Uzi from the 1980s, and several handguns in various calibers. Each weapon was ready for whatever combat situation Angel Jack might encounter while on the run as a wanted fugitive.

Angel Jack found Ethan slouched in a chair with a couple of empty coffee cups on the small table in front of him. Lilly took the two new coffees and put them on the table as she said in a huffy voice, "Drink 'em." Lilly was not normally the bossy type, as her Native American heritage had taught her that men were to be respected, honored, and obeyed. Her gentle spirit was in contrast to Ethan's angry, defensive persona, which caused their twenty-year marriage to have seen its ups and downs, but for the most part, they made a good team. Lilly as the support person and Ethan always taking the lead was what most people expected of them. But today, Lilly's anger overruled her quiet spirit and dictated that she be in charge. She was tired of Ethan's drunken binges!

"You must not get drunk very often," teased Angel Jack.

Ethan took a sip of the fresh coffee and replied, "I usually have a couple of beers a day, but hard liquor messes me up. I ought to know better…"

"So, why did you get sloppy drunk?" queried Angel Jack.

"You know, my best friend in the world died of snake bites trying to protect Nancy Choi, and to put it bluntly, I miss the USA and hate what Clark Johnson and his bunch have done with all this Red-Blue stuff. I tried to talk to them and make some recommendations, but they just nodded in agreement, ignored everything I said, and never called me back—liars! I see the destruction they have caused these past three years, and I'm sick of it!"

Lilly interjected, "How could they have called you back with those earthquakes? Come on, Ethan, be reasonable!"

Angel Jack had taken the seat directly across from Ethan and looked right into his blue eyes as she said slowly, "I believe the time for reason is past...it's time for action!"

"Please explain yourself," said Ethan.

"How many dedicated patriots are in the Misfits?" asked Angel Jack.

"Oh, let's see...we had about 40,000 before the earthquakes. Some of them are helping in the clean-up efforts, and many of them just gave up," said a discouraged Ethan. Just vocalizing his loss of manpower and command made Ethan scan the room for a drink. His heavy drinking was rooted in many bitter disappointments, but this was the hardest to accept. He had loved being the Misfit leader, and it had made him feel superior for the first time in his life. His medium stature and common appearance had made him fodder for all the bullies in his early life. The harsh words and physical abuse by his peers still visited his dreams and clothed his insecurities. Only alcohol medicated the deep pain.

"How many armed patriots could you raise to put this country back together?" queried Angel Jack.

"Maybe 20,000 with serious armaments and transportation. Why do you ask?" quizzed Ethan.

"Maybe your wife didn't tell you who I am. I'm Angel Jack, the one who killed that worthless Kennedy Watson, and I have a plan to take this country back," said the assassin with a resolute stare.

"I'm sorry, I told him, but he was too drunk to remember," explained Lilly.

"That's not important now," said Angel Jack. "What is important is raising a tenacious army of patriots to work my plan and re-boot the USA. Would you like to hear my ideas?"

CHAPTER 16

The Plan

For the last few years, Angel Jack had been formulating a plan to destroy the Red and Blue Nations. She had decided that the key to bringing the old America back hinged upon the ability to "take down" the shared infrastructure of both nations. As Angel Jack's hack of the Red Nation's finances had proven, the infrastructure of both nations depended heavily on electronics to survive. All governmental agencies, manufacturing facilities, shopping areas, and the military relied on electronic systems to operate. Every one of these systems couldn't operate without electricity—plain and simple, electricity like the kind that is available in every American home.

Electricity was discovered by Benjamin Franklin, but the generation and distribution of electricity were first instituted by Thomas Edison. Both of these men would be totally amazed at modern society's dependence upon electrical power. Almost everything anyone does in our technical society is powered by generated electricity. Take down electrical distribution, and the Red and Blue Nations would crumble. Angel Jack had considered these facts carefully and woven them into the plan she called "Bring Back America."

Ethan and Lilly listened in amazement as Angel Jack shared the basics of "Bring Back America." Lilly pondered the strategies Angel Jack presented as she considered what one nation would look like after all the years of division and powerplay. Could anyone ever "bring back" a country that had been so violated and abused by preachers and politicians who had forced their will on the unsuspecting people of America? As her "Misfit" blood began to boil, she quickly refocused her attention on Angel Jack—hopefully—the agent of change.

Angel Jack explained, "Electricity is generated by nuclear, hydro, solar, and even a few coal-burning plants. Each plant feeds into a national power grid where the various utility companies collectively furnish electricity to states and municipalities. Then local entities sell energy to individual customers. The whole system is interconnected. If one area loses power for whatever reason, the grid will automatically redistribute electricity to furnish the supply needed to the area that was disabled. The grid is connected by a system of electronic switches that can send a flow of electricity to any part of the land."

The deadliest disruption factor for this grid is an electromagnetic pulse or EMP that would wreak havoc with any systems that used microchip-based switches. The USA had experienced an EMP attack during the Jihad War years ago when a group of terrorists had exploded a small multi-stage nuclear device above New York City. The tonnage of the bomb was quite minor, but the enhanced EMP waves shut down New York City and portions of New England for a week.

After the war was over, the federal government, working with the power-producing companies, moved swiftly to bolster protection for the electronic switching system. The computer hardware for each electronic switch was encapsulated inside EMP-safe rooms. The safe rooms were located at each power plant, substation, and local distribution point. Each individual cluster of switches was protected by a compartment made of a new aluminum/lead compound called sentinium. A safe room made from this new metallurgical alloy would totally neutralize any electromagnetic pulses that came from an outside attack. Even the cooling systems for the safe rooms were constructed of sentinium encapsulated ductwork. The Red and Blue Nations considered these vital systems to be completely safeguarded. They were wrong.

Angel Jack had cultivated a convenient friendship with Dr. Walaa Amjad, the principal scientist that developed sentinium, the lead-infused aluminum compound used as safe room enclosures. Amjad was an Iranian national that had immigrated to the States after the Jihad War.

Angel Jack had met Amjad at a conference in France. As the foremost presenter in the metallurgical field, Amjad expounded his theories based on years of study and expertise to a captivated audience. With some chicanery, Angel Jack arranged for a seat next to Amjad after the original guest occupying the seat came down with a sudden and violent case of a "stomach virus" that was actually caused by a small vile of toxin that Angel Jack kept in her handbag for just such an occasion. Angel Jack and Dr. Amjad laughed, shared way too much Calvados brandy, and talked about the future. The plight of Amjad's wife and family became the major subject after the Calvados began to talk.

Amjad's work with EMP protection was widely recognized as groundbreaking, but the government procured his work under the War Powers Act and gave Amjad what he considered to be little compensation or recognition.

"Please tell me about your family," Angel Jack probed. "Are they here with you enjoying the beauty of France?"

"No! They wait hopelessly in the ravaged homeland of Iran because the Americans broke their promise. They assured me wealth, prestige, and the relocation of my family to America after certain achievements. I did my job and more, but they reneged on all of their promises!"

Walaa Amjad was angry and offended and swore revenge. It was just the right amount of frustration for Angel Jack to use in her ploy to destroy the Red and Blue Nations. Angel Jack suggested a private breakfast with Dr. Amjad the next morning. "I have a proposition for you regarding a private research facility where you will receive every dream fulfilled for you and your family."

Angel Jack used a portion of her vast fortune obtained as an assassin to construct a state-of-the-art metallurgical lab for Amjad. The doctor had invented the lead-fused aluminum compound he called sentinium because it acts as a sentry against EMP attacks, including attacks from the "Super-EMP" weapons developed by the Chinese and Russians in the 2020s. Since sentinium was a superb shield against electromagnetic pulses, Amjad had to figure out a way to attack his own "child," his creation. None of the conventional means of cutting metal could even scratch sentinium as the molecular structure was impervious to plasma or oxyacetylene equipment. Amjad had created the new compound to resist damage, and now he would have to find a way to "kill his own baby."

While Dr. Amjad worked on a device that would quickly cut through sentinium, Angel Jack had contracted with the Tactical Military Drone Company, TMDC, Inc., to construct a delivery system for whatever Dr. Amjad designed. It was decided that the drones would attack as a group, with each drone delivering a yet-to-be-designed super laser burst that would attack the walls of sentinium. These attacks would tear down the integrity of the alloy's superstructure from the inside out. TMDC had no idea they were dealing with the notorious Angel Jack. She had presented herself as an attaché of Admiral Choi, who was looking for drones to attack a new form of a Chinese tank. Angel Jack thought that assuming the identity of someone who worked for her sister was not only exceedingly clever but great fun!

While Dr. Amjad and TMDC worked on their related projects, Ethan and Lilly James began to quietly lay the groundwork for their Repatriation Army. Many of the Misfits had spurned electronic communication for old short-wave radio systems like truckers used in the last century. The Misfits also used the names of "make-believe teenagers" to communicate in code on social media. Ethan's make-believe teen, or MBT, as the Misfits referred to them, was Mikey Donald. Mikey's social media pages were full of pictures and events that didn't really exist, but if Mikey announced a party, all the Misfits knew a meeting was being planned. Mikey had over 10,000 social media friends on various platforms, and all of them were "make-believe teens."

After three months of working eighteen-hour days, Dr. Amjad finally found a way to cut through sentinium. He developed a new type of super laser that burned much hotter and could rapidly cut through two inches of sentinium. The super laser generators had a range of about ten meters, but the bursts would be deployed by the drones extremely close to the sentinium targets. He was able to interface with the TMDC-designed drones to house his new super laser cutting device. The TMDC drones were a common site within the two nations, as drone sentries and weaponized drones were used to protect sensitive industrial and military sites. Therefore, Angel Jack's drones would attract little attention.

When Angel Jack was advised that the drones were ready to be tested on a live target, she chose a little out-of-the-way substation in Ty Ty, Georgia. The substation was thousands of miles from the real target and would serve as a demonstration of Angel Jack's diabolical scheme.

Around 2 a.m. on December 2nd, a nondescript transfer truck pulled into Ty Ty, Georgia, and parked in a pecan orchard just off exit 35 on Interstate 75. "Well, Doc, I hope your super laser proves to be everything you promised," said Angel Jack with a smirk.

"Of course, it will," snaped Amjad. "You knew I was the best when you asked me to take down these fake American nations. There is no Red or Blue, just America, with its injustice and prejudice toward people of Arab descent. Release the drones and watch my genius at work!" railed Amjad.

The GPS location of the substation was downloaded into the drones, and their cameras were activated. With Angel Jack and Dr. Amjad working the controls, the drones were released to fly the short five-mile distance to the substation. The drone cameras sent a perfect inflight picture back to the command module. These drones were not the old propeller type that could fly at about 100 mph, but the new jet-propelled drones could achieve speeds of over 500 miles per hour, the speed of a commercial airliner.

Five drones flew over the substation razor wire-protected fence and headed straight for the small building that housed the substation switches within the sentinium encasement. The lead drone was equipped with tools for "breaking and entering" and proceeded to saw off the padlock and open the door with its mechanical arm. The basketball-sized drones entered the room and began to attack the casing with multiple laser bursts. Within a minute, the sentinium shell had been breached, and the drone carrying the electromagnetic generator released a low humming pulse that permanently disabled the switches and plunged the little community of Ty Ty into darkness.

Angel Jack cackled into the blackness, "Well done, boys. Now let's create more of you drones, build an army, and take down those two illegitimate nations!

CHAPTER 17

Opposites Really Do Attract!

As Charles Sikes sat at the table by himself while Maria was in the lady's room, his thoughts turned to his childhood and, of course, to Maria. After Maria had saved Charles' life on the riverboat during the deadly earthquakes, she sat with him every night while he was in the hospital recovering from his wounds. This night out was billed as a "thank you dinner" to the woman who had saved his life, but Charles knew it was more. Could they make a relationship work? Charles didn't know, but he was sure willing to try!

At ten years of age, Charles Sikes was already an entrepreneur. His lemonade stand, off Highland Avenue on the outskirts of Wichita, Kansas, was a huge hit with the soccer moms shuttling their children back and forth to the various athletic fields. The kids were always thirsty after their matches, and Charles' fifty cents/cup lemonade was cheaper than a soda at a fast-food restaurant. So, Charles could usually clear $20 every day he set up his stand. He had constructed the stand out of half-inch PVC pipe and cardboard boxes and could load the contraption on his little brother's wagon and haul it behind his bike.

Charles' little business was thriving until the day Teddy Garr and his little band of thugs came calling. It had been a particularly good business day for Charles, and he was busy loading the stand components onto the wagon when he felt a tremendous shove that knocked him onto the concrete curb between the sidewalk and the street. As Charles sat up and looked in the direction of the shove, he received a kick to the face that knocked him over the curb and into the asphalt street. The original fall hadn't done much damage, but the second attack had bloodied Charles' nose and put a huge scrape on his face. Even though Charles was dazed, he could see twelve-year-old Teddy and the boys throwing his stand components into the street. As Charles slowly got to his feet, the boys began to run away laughing, and he heard Teddy say tauntingly, "Hey, little businessman, we got your money! Sucka! Haha!"

Through his embarrassment and pain, Charles called out after Teddy, "Hey, big guy...you better be nice to me!"

"And why should I do that?" asked Teddy jeeringly.

"Because one day you'll be working for me," shouted Charles.

Teddy and his little gang of ruffians just laughed and sped off.

Just as Charles reached for his pocket to retrieve his cell phone and call his dad, Mrs. Smith, his next-door neighbor, spotted Charles and stopped to give aid. Mrs. Smith and her two eight-year-old twins helped Charles retrieve his broken stand, wagon, and bike and put them in the back of her van. She dropped off Charles in his driveway and helped him unload his stuff before saying, "Charles, you should ask your dad to call the cops on that little band of thugs! They need to be stopped!" Charles thanked Mrs. Smith and then limped into the house, where he fell sobbing into his father's arms.

Charles' dad, Myron Sikes, was the Trinity Baptist Church's lead pastor. Myron was a big man but knew how to be gentle. He held the sobbing Charles for several minutes until the boy regained his composure and shared the story with his dad. After a long pause, Myron spoke, "Charles, those boys really did you dirty. They destroyed your lemonade stand, stole your money, and hurt you physically and emotionally. They certainly deserve to be punished, but I think we should try a little 'spiritual experiment' in this situation."

"Experiment. What experiment?" said a bewildered Charles.

"Let's call on the Lord in this situation, son. Romans 12:19 says, 'Dear friends, never take revenge. Leave that to the righteous anger of God. For the Scriptures say, "I will take revenge; I will pay them back," says the Lord.' Let's forgive Teddy and the other boys and see if this scripture is really true. Whadaya say?" said Myron with a smile.

Charles was silent for a couple of minutes as he considered his dad's proposition, then he bowed his head and said, "Father God, I forgive Teddy and his gang and ask You to fix this situation. I trust You and place my life in Your hands.... Amen!" Myron then gathered Charles up into a big bear hug, and they both laughed and cried at the same time. Teddy and his gang were arrested a few weeks later after they were caught trying to break into a local hardware store. Myron planned to visit them and present the gospel while they were incarcerated in the Regional Youth Detention Center. It seemed the Lord's vengeance was working.

Charles first met Maria when they were both attending Eastwood Junior High School. Maria's dad had recently been stationed at McConnell Air Force Base just outside of Wichita. Major Cortez was in charge of the Stratotankers refueling squadron. It was a great career move for Major Cortez, but just another physical move for Maria and her siblings. Maria had attended four different elementary schools, and this was her second junior high school in as many years. Maria felt like she had no permanent friends, and therefore, she guarded her heart against any close relationships.

Maria came in the middle of the school year and was assigned to Mrs. Battle's homeroom and was given a desk on the second row, right behind Charles. Maria and Charles also had American history class together, where, once again, Maria found herself seated right behind Charles. Charles sat on the front row in front of Mr. Benson, the history teacher, and Maria could tell immediately that Charles had a very quick mind but was also Mr. Benson's "pet." Charles not only answered most of the questions but even asked additional questions. This made many of the other kids groan because they knew Charles would ace all the tests and make them look bad. "Charlie smarty pants," as Maria called him, made her want to puke. When Charles would ask additional questions, Maria would make a little gagging sound just loud enough for Charles to hear.

As class was being dismissed one day, Charles turned around, looked her dead in the eye, and said, "So, what's with all that gagging, señorita?"

Maria ignored the obvious racial slur toward her Mexican heritage and said, "You see, Charlie smarty pants, when you answer all the questions and then ask your own dumb questions, it makes me want to puke! Actually, sometimes I throw up in my mouth a little, and that's the gagging you hear."

Charles had never had anyone talk to him like that. After all, he was a straight-A student, class president, and part of the eighth-grade debate team. Charles simply gathered his books, got up, and quickly walked out the door.

The next day in history class, Charles was not seated in front of Maria. He had swapped seats with another boy and was now seated on the far-left end of the front row. Charles still answered quite a few questions but didn't ask any of his own. As Maria saw Charles from her new vantage point, she noticed that he was good-looking, with light brown hair and a nice profile. She kept glancing over at him during class and also noticed how well-spoken he was when he did answer a question. Hmmm. Maybe she did come on a little strong yesterday.

When class was over, Maria stepped right in front of Charles and said, "Hey, Charles, I think we got off on the wrong foot yesterday." Charles ignored her and started toward the door. Maria grabbed him by the arm and said, "Please, Charles, I'm trying to apologize..." Charles' body language softened, and he faced Maria.

After an awkward silence, Charles said, "That's okay. Say, do you want to go to the eighth-grade spring dance with me Friday night?"

Maria heard herself say, "Sure!" They quickly exchanged phone numbers, and Charles left for his next class while Maria, still standing in the history classroom, wondered what had just happened.

The eighth-grade spring dance was held in the school gym. This was the one occasion of the year where the faculty required the students to dress up. Charles' dad drove him over to the base housing, where they picked up Maria. Major Cortez and his wife Naomi met Charles at the front door and invited him to sit in the den while Maria finished getting ready. Major Cortez waved for Myron to come in, too, and Myron sat with Charles, the major, and Naomi until they heard Maria coming down the stairs. The adults and Charles stood when Maria made her "grand entrance." Charles gulped when he saw Maria as the adults gushed over her appearance. Maria did look lovely in her lavender party dress and stacked heels. Her trim figure and long dark hair were accentuated by her beautifully tan skin and radiant smile. Charles just stood there looking bewildered until Myron said, "Hey, son, don't you have something for Maria?" Charles robotically extended a corsage made of delicate white rosebuds synched together with lavender ribbons. Thankfully, Naomi offered to pin the corsage on Maria's dress.

Charles relaxed at the dance, and he and Maria had a blast dancing, talking, and laughing. Myron took the two happy teens back to Maria's house after the dance, and Charles held Maria's hand as they walked to the front door. Charles tightened back up as he stood with Maria on the porch. He thought about kissing her, but his dad was watching, and he had never kissed anyone before anyway. Finally, Maria stood on her tip toes and kissed Charles on the cheek. Then they both whispered good night, and she slipped inside the front door.

Charles' thoughts were interrupted by Maria coming back to the table. He stood and pulled the chair out for her and noticed how attractive her tan shoulders and dark hair were. Charles seated himself and then poured a glass of champagne for both of them. He then gazed across the table and saw that wonderfully radiant smile and those dancing brown eyes and said slowly, "Maria, there's something I want to talk to you about..."

CHAPTER 18

Double Strike

Lilly and Ethan had organized a camping bikers convention that would meet outside Washington, D. C., close to Prince William Forest Park. They had rented a twenty-acre plot of private land adjacent to the park that would accommodate the tents and supplies for their convention. The brochure promised an appearance by Flowing River, a popular new country band from Nashville, Tennessee.

Actually, there was no convention or country band, but there were 1,000 bikers prepared to attack governmental buildings in the D. C. area that furnished administrative support for the Red and Blue Nations. The bikers brought small arms, grenades, and a few grenade launchers to attack the facilities. The goal was not to actually destroy anything but to stage a national distraction that would attract military activity and furnish a "smokescreen" for Angel Jack's real target—the huge substation that served the north side of Dallas, including Clark's compound. Plus, the standby generators at Clark's compound would also be put out of service by a separate group of drones. The attack on D. C. was scheduled for dawn on August 4th, while the Dallas substation and compound generators would be attacked at 2 a.m. CST the next morning.

The 1,000 bikers roared onto the rented twenty-acre plot on August the 3rd and began setting up their tents for the supposed convention. There was country music playing over loudspeakers and vendors selling food and drink for the fake convention that was to start the next day. The bikers set up their tents and checked their early morning agenda as well as their weapons. The ruse was working perfectly.

At 5 a.m. on August 4th, 400 of the bikers designated as Repatriation Strike Forces pulled out of the campground and headed toward Washington, D. C. The bikers, now broken up into twenty groups of twenty riders, left in five-minute intervals and took different routes into the city. The remaining would-be-campers packed up everything and left the area as quickly as possible.

The twenty targets that had been chosen housed important support facilities for the Red and Blue Nations. The Internal Revenue Service building on Constitution Avenue was first on the list to be hit. Angel Jack had planned to simultaneously attack the twenty targets right at 6 a.m. when the city streets were almost bare, and the protection services for the targets were changing shifts. The first group of twenty riders broke through the barricades and quickly overcame the few guards at the facility. The riders were not only noisy but had donned black tactical gear that would give them some protection against small arms fire. While a few of the riders engaged the guards, the others drove in circles around the building while firing small arms and launching grenades at the building. The weapons did little damage to the building but did serve as a wake-up call for the D. C. protection services, police, and military. The Fort McNair Army base was notified after the first few shots were fired, and they scrambled a team of rangers in the direction of the IRS building. By the time additional help had arrived, the damage was done, and the bikers had roared off into the early morning light.

This attack plan was repeated concurrently over the next hour in nineteen more locations. A few fires had been set, but there was no heavy damage, plus the perpetrators were leaving the city via twenty different routes. Not a single Repatriation Force member had been killed or captured, but the city was stunned. Early morning workers shot videos of the attacks from their cell phones and sent those videos to the major news outlets. It appeared the city had been under serious attack at twenty different locations, and the D. C. police, the Secret Service, and the military were all assessing the situation and bracing for more attacks. Angel Jack's plan of confusion and fear had worked perfectly.

The D. C. attacks had intrigued the whole country. Both news agencies and Red and Blue officials filled the holovision displays as they attempted to figure out what was going on. Clark and the Red and Blue Nations leaders were calling for calm, but privately, they were perplexed at the attacks. In one of the Red Blue staff meetings, Nancy Choi gave her assessment of the situation when she said, "Okay, everyone, listen to me. These attacks were not real but classic diversionary tactics. I expect the real reason for these attacks will be revealed soon. I am putting the military on high alert. And Clark, I suggest you double the guard at the compound."

Clark said, "Yes, ma'am" in his lazy drawl and then excused himself from the meeting to go play with Little Clark.

Angel Jack's semitrailer rig was already parked at an overnight truck stop a few miles from Clark's Christian Nationalist compound. The compound served as the home base for the Red and Blue Nations' base of operations as well as Clark's gigantic ministry headquarters. Angel Jack moved the rig out of the truck stop parking lot and traveled down a dirt road to a small plot of pastureland. The land was deserted and was perfect for Angel Jack's wicked needs. Dr. Amjad stayed at the lab, but Angel Jack had brought three of her bodyguards with her to guard the rig while she prepared to release the drones.

Sheltered by a starless night, the guards unpacked the crates that held the gray metallic, basketball-sized drones and put all twenty on the sandy earth. At exactly 2 a.m., Angel Jack launched the drones into the blackness and followed their flight on the video screens attached to the flight operations console. Fifteen of the drones headed toward the large substation that fed electricity to the compound, while the other five raced toward the generators that provided emergency power for the compound in the event of a power outage. Angel Jack wiped the perspiration from her forehead and sighed softly as her destructive dream unfolded. "It's really happening. Clark Johnson, that arrogant little preacher, is about to pay!"

The fifteen drones designated, A Group flew into the substation in tight formation and then separated to do their individual jobs. The substation had three separate switching rooms that contained electronic devices protected by sentinium enhanced structures. The "wrecker drones" cut the metal locks from the switch room doors with a buzzing sound and the plasma drones began invading the sentinium walls to expose the electronic switch gear. When all three switch clusters were visible, the EMP drones released a burst of energy that permanently disabled the switch gear. The Christian Nationalist compound and 400,000 homes and businesses in Dallas were thrown into total darkness. After a few seconds, the emergency generators at the compound fired up, but the darkness once again cloaked the compound as the drones in B Group rendered the generators ineffective.

*****

Julianne was awakened by the black stillness and quiet warmth of the evening. She retrieved her cell phone and turned on the flashlight before calling out to Seth.

"Hey, sweetheart, what's going on?" said Seth as he sat up and drowsily rubbed his eyes.

"There's something very wrong, Seth. The power is off, and the emergency generators are not responding. What could be wrong?" asked a frightened Julianne. Little Clark began crying, and Julianne went over to pick him up while Seth quickly put on his jeans and running shoes.

"You stay here with Little Clark while I go check this out," said Seth as he headed for the door. As Seth walked out into the hall, he stumbled into Clark, who was about to knock on their door.

"Clark, what's going on?" asked Seth. Before Clark could answer, both their cell phones rang with a joint call from the chief of security, Captain Lee Baker.

"Gentlemen get your families to the safe room and meet me at Security Command pronto!" exclaimed Captain Baker.

Clark and Seth quickly retrieved the tactical flashlights from the nearby emergency supply closet and
ushered Julianne and Little Clark to the safe room at
the end of the hall. Then they rapidly walked down the
two flights of stairs to the Security Command center.
Captain Baker and his company commanders were using the light from their flashlights and cell phones to
navigate the totally dark room. The main cameras that
protected the complex were up and running on their
battery packs. The cameras fed signals to the monitoring computers, which in turn projected the images
onto several large screens, which also were served by
battery packs. The screens showed a grouping of about
fifty figures in tactical garb set up at each exit way. The
soldiers were taking shelter behind the huge trees and
landscape boulders that decorated the four exits. They
not only had weapons but also were equipped with
acetylene torches and metal saws that would be used to
breach the compound doors.

Seth asked the obvious question, "How long will the
battery packs last?"

"The computers can last up to forty-eight hours, but
the cameras are only good for twenty-four hours. However, I have put the cameras on a rotating service cycle
that will save enough battery life to add a few hours of
selective camera viewing to the system," said Captain
Baker.

"What is this all about?" asked Clark.

"We really don't know yet...but these figures appear to be soldiers of some sort. Apparently, they plan to breach this compound. We only have 125 armed men here at the present time, but I have contacted the Dallas Police Department and also sent an emergency text to Admiral Choi. We should have help in the near future," said Captain Baker. "Until then," continued Baker, "get the most vulnerable people into the safe rooms and arm everyone else that knows how to fight."

CHAPTER 19

Romance Put on Hold

Charles told Maria that he had deep feelings for her and wanted to date her on a serious basis. Maria responded that she had loved him since junior high but had been put off by his ridiculously conservative political views. Charles laughed at that statement and said that if Seth and Julianne could make it, they could too. Maria and Charles both smiled and then shared a tender kiss right there in the restaurant. Their differences were even reflected in the meals they ordered at this swanky D. C. restaurant. His choice was rare, aged ribeye steak, loaded baked potato and green beans in leu of a sissy salad, as he called it. His mid-America roots permeated every bite. Her choice of sautéed fresh salmon with dill sauce, quinoa, and a fruit and arugula salad with light lemon vinaigrette reflected her international travel and healthy eating habits. Opposites do attract, but as Charles's father, Reverend Myron Sikes, used to say, "The number one ingredient in a healthy marriage is always hard work." There would be a lot of hard work in this relationship. The soft flickering candlelight defied the sinister Dallas events scheduled in only a few short hours...if life were only simple and love could be fulfilled.

Because of the attacks of the day, Charles had escorted Maria back to her D. C. apartment with both of their secret service units in tow. He returned to his own luxury apartment and sat down to study reports of the early morning attacks. He had just dozed off when suddenly he was awakened by the sound of his cell phone playing the emergency tone. Charles quickly answered the call to find an excited Clark on the other end of the line. Clark explained the situation at the Dallas compound and advised Charles and Maria to double up on their secret service units and get to the local safe house as quickly as possible. Maria had received a similar call from Seth, and both prime ministers arrived at the safe house within the hour.

*****

Angel Jack had never intended to harm anyone in the complex; she merely wanted to keep the compound paralyzed until she could force her demands upon the Red and Blue Nations. There was no actual communication between the compound personnel and the Repatriation Forces (RF) during the first twenty-four hours. Captain Baker and a small force of elite commandos attempted to break through the RF lines about dawn, but they were beaten back by small arms fire and tear gas. After Baker and his men were driven back inside, the RF barricaded all four exits by sealing the doors shut using acetylene torches and welding equipment. It became obvious that the RF was not trying to break in but keep the compound residents trapped inside. This was not an attack on the compound but rather a siege.

After the second day, everything on the backup battery pack ceased to operate, and since all refrigeration and air conditioning was out of operation, the 300 permanent compound inhabitants sweltered in the heat and were only eating dry or canned food. On the third day, Angel Jack cut the water off.

The military and Dallas police had both attempted to rescue the compound residents, but fifteen additional EMP drones had formed a domed perimeter that took out every vehicle, helicopter, and communication device that came within 1,000 yards of the compound. Plus, the cell phones of the residents had been jammed within the first few hours. The situation looked hopeless.

Admiral Choi had set up a command post about twenty miles away in a part of Dallas that still had power. While Nancy and her advisors brainstormed concerning possible solutions to the situation, suddenly, her private phone line rang.

"This is Admiral Choi," Nancy said in her monotone military voice.

"Well, hello, big sister!" said Angel Jack with thick sarcasm.

"How did you get this number?" demanded Nancy.

"Aw, c'mon, sis, is that really important? What is important is that I cut the water off a few hours ago, and your friends could be dying of heat exhaustion about now," said Angel Jack with a sneer.

"Okay, AJ, what are your demands?" said Nancy.

"My demands are simple, big sister. I want you to stand down while my forces instruct the compound people to lay down all arms and prepare to leave the compound and come outside, while my people go inside," said Angel Jack.

"So, what's your purpose in all this?" said Nancy.

"It's simple, sis! My Repatriation Forces are going to resurrect the good ol' USA, and to do that, we must capture the data from the Red and Blue computer servers. Therefore, we will open the main entrance and allow all the good people to come out that exit while my forces enter the service entrance and procure the necessary server modules."

Nancy agreed to stand down all her forces, and Angel Jack sent her a drone-delivered sat phone that was not affected by the jamming frequency. She also supplied a sat phone to the compound by having a drone drop it down through a vent pipe. Nancy went to communicate with her troops while Angel Jack had her welding team work to remove welded seals to the main gate and service doors. The besieged residents of the compound retrieved the sat phone and were told to move toward the main entrance, where they would be extracted ten at a time. However, Angel Jack had no idea that a plan had been prepared for just such a crisis.

"Is that everybody, Captain Baker?" asked Clark.

"They have all been given a protein bar and a bottle of water from the stock you had saved in the emergency storage area. I must say, sir, that was a brilliant idea to store food and water in a facility that had its own utility system," said Baker.

"Actually, Captain, it wasn't very brilliant at all. I come from a part of the South known as 'Tornado Alley.' All of the families in that area stored food and water in anticipation of the tornadoes that would rumble through every so often. Most of us had a little portable generator that would keep our refrigerators going too. We might have been rustic, but we were ready!" said Clark with a smile.

The three hundred permanent residents of the compound moved into a twenty-foot-wide tunnel that would carry them to safety. They were transported by oversized golf carts down the 1.2-mile tunnel to the secret exit in the fake maintenance building that was set up for that very purpose. A portion of Nancy's troops were waiting at the end of the tunnel to extract the 300 souls. Also, the technicians had removed the memory storage modules from the servers and carried them into the safety of the tunnel.

The escape tunnel was Seth's idea. Before Clark's compound was expanded to include the executive offices of the Red and Blue Nations, Seth had approached Clark and the other leaders about the idea of an escape tunnel. It took nine months of work using special mining equipment to dig and prepare the tunnel, but the hard work and expense had certainly paid off today. Even though the inhabitants of the compound had given up their normal lifestyle for a few days, they had helped trick Angel Jack into revealing her real plans. Now they could "escape" into the tunnel and let Captain Baker and his men do their job.

When Angel Jack's thirty commandoes broke through the service entrance doors and rushed into the building to seize the server memory pods, they found the building totally empty and the memory pods gone. The captain of the commandoes called Angel Jack and said, "Ma'am, you're not going to believe this, but everybody's gone, and the memory pods have been removed from the servers."

"Get your men out, Captain! This is obviously a trap!" screamed Angel Jack. But before the men could retrace their steps, Captain Baker's elite security team burst out of hiding with guns blazing. A few of the commandoes chose to stay and fight but the majority headed for the exterior doors. Four of Angel Jack's men were killed, six were wounded, and the others threw down their weapons and surrendered. None of the elite security team members suffered a scratch.

Angel Jack was beaten, and she knew it.

Nancy rang Angel Jack's sat phone, and she answered, "Hello, you witch of a sister!"

"How does it feel to be beaten and humiliated by the person you hate the most, AJ?" asked Nancy. There was no reply from Angel Jack, and then Nancy saw her mini jet-copter speeding toward the West. Nancy smiled to herself as she thought of the defeat and humiliation that she had just inflicted on her half-sister, the assassin.

Today, the compound was saved, but one day they would meet again, face to face.

CHAPTER 20

Let's Go Ahead and Do This!

Charles and Maria were extremely happy about the news that the compound and the Red Blue Team were safe. They were also excited about expressing their true feelings for each other. After they got the good report concerning their friends in Dallas, they sat in the small breakfast room of the safe house and had a celebratory cup of coffee with blueberry scones.

After some friendly chatter, Charles paused and looked Maria right in the eyes.

"Maria," he began, "I have loved you since the night of our junior high dance, and I know you love me too, so let's get married!"

Maria let out a high-pitched laugh and said, "If you're not teasing, I'm all for it!"

Charles walked around the table, gave her a long hug, and then kissed her passionately. They held each other for a few minutes until Maria said, "Charles, I want to marry you but with three conditions. I want Clark to do the wedding, I want us to talk to Julianne and Seth about how to make this marriage work, and I want you to buy me a huge diamond engagement ring!"

Charles threw his head back and laughed and said, "I certainly agree with all three! Now, let's get dressed and go ring shopping!"

*****

Charles opened the door for Maria, and they entered "Always Jewelers," a premier jewelry store in the D. C. area. The secret service men agreed to stay outside if the owner locked the store down while Charles and Maria shopped. Arrangements had been made for the store to be empty of other customers at 11 a.m. that day. It wasn't every day that the prime ministers of two nations went ring shopping.

Maria enjoyed dressing up for special events and always looked elegant but at ease around any guest or dignitaries she might mingle with. She did have a love affair with jewelry and wanted something special for her engagement ring. They shopped loose diamonds for about an hour until Maria found a pear-shaped three-carat pink diamond of excellent quality. Pink stones of this size are rare and pricey, but Charles had said that money was no object, so she said with a tinkle in her voice, "Charles, I want that one!" The jeweler affirmed their choice and moved them over to the settings only counter to complete their design.

*****

The Dallas Emerald Hotel at Park Place was chosen for the wedding venue. With its 1200 rooms, huge ballrooms, and close proximity to the Dallas/Fort Worth International Airport, The Emerald, as the locals called it, was one of the most beautiful and technologically savvy hotels in the world. Many foreign dignitaries were expected to attend, and their security teams would be able to tap into The Emerald security system as an added feature in keeping their people safe.

Marie and Charles had been meeting with Seth and Julianne on a regular basis for over a month. Clark had input as the wedding officiant, but they felt Seth and Julianne could give them the most advice regarding their political differences in a Red/Blue marriage.

Charles and Maria took a seat on the large sofa in Seth and Julianne's suite. Julianne, who had just completed her daily run on the treadmill in the hotel's workout room, was having her normal "after run" green tea. She asked the others if they cared for a snack or something to drink. Maria and Charles declined, but Seth began brewing a cappuccino on the hotel's in-house machine. While Seth worked, he asked the two "lovebirds," as Clark called them, to tell him what they spoke of the last time they were together. Charles said, "You gave us those personality tests that defined our distinctive characteristics. We discovered that we sure are different!"

Maria chimed in, "I guess opposites really do attract!"

"Actually," said Seth, "opposites complete what their spouse might be missing. Julianne's gentleness and compassion allow people to open up without fear, while my boldness and leadership skills allow me to teach them how to succeed. We are an unbeatable team!"

Julianne spoke up, "So let me ask you a question. What is the number one ingredient in a healthy marriage? Now, remember that I said 'healthy marriage' not 'good or bad' marriage. Even a healthy person gets sick sometimes, but they get well with proper care. So, what is the number one ingredient in a healthy marriage?"

Maria immediately responded, "Love and forgiveness!"

After a couple of moments, Charles said, "A relationship with Christ?"

Julianne said, "All those ingredients are good, but they are not the number one ingredient...the number one ingredient in a healthy marriage is *hard work*. A marriage is a living organism, and it must be maintained and cared for like any other precious commodity. My favorite example is a swimming pool. When we first get a new pool, it is beautiful and crystal clear. Everyone is so excited to see it and attend our pool parties. However, if we don't maintain that new pool with cleaning and the proper chemicals, it will quickly get dark and ugly. Microscopic organisms can multiply and overtake a beautiful pool in no time. So, it is with marriage. Microscopic offenses and annoying habits intrude and pollute a healthy marriage. It takes work and maintenance to keep a marriage a thing of beauty."

✳ ✳ ✳ ✳ ✳

The news of the upcoming nuptials had leaked to the general public months before the announcement was planned, and many of the Red Nation and Blue Nation citizens were unhappy. Protestors from both nations gathered outside the Emerald to display their displeasure. Shrieks of "Traitor, we trusted you" billowed above the noise of the motorcade carrying Maria and Charles, the wedding party, and the massive security force. Once the motorcade entered the designated section of the underground garage, the protestors were left behind.

Charles gently held Maria's hand as the elevator ascended to the ballroom, where they would become Mr. and Mrs. Cortez-Sikes. Through all the chaos, Charles' mind wandered to the upcoming night they would share together. The imaginations and dreams of intimacy and fulfilled love that he had nurtured through the years were about to become a reality for Charles. Maria brushed her bangs, touched the pearls around her neck, and wondered if her makeup was picture-perfect. The elevator dinged, the doors opened, and the couple released hands and made their way to the separate dressing parlors.

The minutes seemed like hours, but the processional, the homily, and the exchange of rings, were now complete, and Clark said with a big grin, "Charles, you may kiss your bride." The ballroom erupted in thunderous applause, joy, and laughter. Charles and Maria were now together at last.

CHAPTER 21

Restructure

Now that the prime ministers of the two nations were married, Clark and Seth stepped in to head up the restructuring of the New USA. A new constitution would have to be written, and even though it would largely be based on the original United States Constitution, a myriad of lawyers plus the original lawmakers from the two nations were being employed to fashion the new document.

Clark was super conservative, and Seth was ultra-liberal, so compromise was the only avenue by which the new documents would be created. The battles were heated and raged far into the night on many occasions. At times it seemed the Red and Blue Nations would stand as they currently existed. Clark became so exasperated one Wednesday evening that he gathered his things and just left without a word. Julianne became so distraught over her father's disappearance that she threatened to take Little Clark and leave Seth.

Clark traveled the ten hours from Dallas to Tupelo, Mississippi, and turned down Hawk Avenue, the street where he spent most of his boyhood. Clark's father had died at only fifty-nine years of age, but Rose, his eighty-four-year-old mother, still lived in the three-bedroom, one-bath home at 224 Hawk Avenue. Clark didn't see his mother often, but they spoke on the phone about once a week, and Clark made sure she lived comfortably and securely. Rose was still very independent but allowed Clark to furnish her with a full-time housekeeper who doubled as a "nurse" when the situation arose.

Clark had borrowed a personal vehicle from Isaac Powell, his chief of security, to make the trip and made Isaac swear that he would not tell anyone where Clark was going. Clark figured that Isaac would crack under pressure as soon as Julianne arranged to question him privately. But until then, Clark was going to visit with his mom and forget about all the wrangling over a new constitution.

Clark had stopped just outside Dallas and bought a pair of sunglasses and a ball cap that said "gone fishing" on the front. He put his coat and tie in the back seat and rolled his sleeves up to the elbow. He paid cash for gas and food and made sure to do the speed limit on I-10 as he traveled across Texas and Louisiana. Clark was sure no one would recognize him, and he was right. His own mother didn't recognize him when he knocked on her front door.

Clark took his sunglasses off and said, "Mama, it's me, Clark!"

Rose stared for a moment and then opened the door and gave Clark a big hug. Once inside, she said, "Clark Johnson, what are you doing here—and with no security? Clark, Julianne's already been kidnapped. Do you want that to happen to you too?"

Clark smiled sheepishly and said, "Aw, Mama, you know the good Lord looks after drunks and fools, so I was counting on that last category, fools, to work for me."

They both laughed heartily, and Rose said, "Okay, son, come sit down, and I'll get you a glass of sweet tea, and you can tell me all about it."

Clark told his mom all about his efforts to work with Seth and the Blue Nation in trying to develop a strong, innovative constitution for the New USA. Finally, Clark said in a frustrated voice, "I don't know why we are doing this anyway. The Red Nation is productive and healthy. I have no idea how I got the notion that we ought to rejoin the two nations."

Rose said softly, "Son, do you remember going on holovision with Seth and telling everyone that the conservatives and liberals needed each other in order to bring balance? I love the Red Nation, but c'mon, son, public hangings?"

"I know you are right, Mama; I've just become tired of the fighting. Do you have any 'Mama wisdom' for your son?"

"Actually, I do, son. Compromise is born out of the belief that the other side has something to offer that will bring balance and stability to a union. The original constitution was born out of months of discussion, compromise, and rewrites. Then all thirteen colonies had to ratify it. How long have you been working, thirty days? Clark, you can do this, but it's gonna take time."

"As usual, you are right again, Mama. I need to hunker down and get this thing done because the liberals and conservatives really do need each other. They need our order and discipline, and we need their compassion. When I first met my sweetheart Olivia, it was her beauty that originally attracted me, but then as our differences emerged, I realized that I needed what she had and who she was to make me whole."

"That's it, son! This rejoining of the two nations is like a married couple trying to live together. The Reds and Blues need each other!"

CHAPTER 22

The Attack

"Please pray with me, Mom. I need the Lord's own strength to follow through with this reunion," said Clark.

Just as Clark and Rose joined hands and bowed their heads in prayer, a rocket-propelled grenade broke through the glass picture window and lodged underneath the solid oak buffet that Rose's dad had given her mother on the day Rose was born. The heavy oak structure of the buffet protected Clark and Rose from the worst part of the blast, but they were still knocked against the wall separating the kitchen from the great room. Even in his stupor, Clark could hear men shouting as they raced toward the front door. Clark had the presence of mind to draw his mid-sized Glock 9mm pistol from his inside the waistband holster. As the men charged toward his door, he wondered if his eight shots would do anything to protect him and his now groaning mother from certain death.

As three men wearing full black combat gear kicked the door in and burst into the great room, a smoke bomb went off in the middle of the room, and Clark felt himself being jerked through the cased opening between the great room and the kitchen. He could see his mom being dragged in the same direction. He caught a glimpse of Admiral Choi and several other "good guys" before they deposited his mother and him into the laundry room and shut the door. Clark glanced over to see Rose awake but in obvious pain. Clark managed to stash his mom beside the washer and dryer and then took position between her and the door as he racked his gun and switched the safety off.

When the shooting started, it was loud and furious but lasted less than thirty seconds. Clark heard some commotion and more gunfire toward the front of the house and gingerly peeked out of the laundry room window to see Nancy and four others attack a black van that was parked on the curb. Three men brandishing automatic weapons came out of the van and were ordered to lay down. One of the men dropped his weapon and immediately laid down on the lawn, but the other two refused to respond to the order and took bullets to the neck above their body armor. With the van now secured, Clark saw Nancy striding swiftly back toward the house and thought, *Uh oh, I'm in more trouble than I would be with the murderers.*

Suddenly the laundry room door burst open, and a fiery-eyed Admiral Nancy Choi towered over Clark as he checked on his mother. "What in God's name did you think you were doing?" said Nancy in a stern, loud voice.

Clark felt like a little boy taking a "chewing" from his third-grade teacher but stammered, "Uh...uh...you're totally right, Nan; I had no business going off alone, even to visit my mom."

Before Nancy could respond, Rose rolled over on her side and spat up a small amount of bright red blood. Nancy immediately called for Kirk, who had some military medical training. Kirk gently searched for puncture wounds but found none and offered that there must be internal injuries caused by the blast. The EMTs had been called before the firefight in anticipation of injuries and arrived within seconds to take Rose to the hospital. As Clark followed the EMTs that were taking his mother to the emergency vehicle, he passed through the great room and surveyed the damage. Pieces of the shattered buffet were strewn about; the windows were blown out, and the bullet-riddled bodies of the three assassins lay crumpled in pools of blood. Clark whispered a prayer of thanks and walked through the hole where the front door used to be and made his way to the emergency vehicle.

As Rose was being carefully positioned into the ambulance, Nancy insisted that she take Clark to the hospital too. It was only then that Clark realized that he had sustained numerous small wounds from oak splinters and broken glass propelled by the explosion. Clark got into the back seat with Kirk while Sonya drove, and Nancy rode "shotgun." As they pulled out of the backyard, Sonya said cheerfully, "Hello, Reverend Johnson!"

"You can drop the reverend title, Sonya. Besides, if you continue to call me reverend, I'll call you former FBI Special Agent Sonya Arthur," said Clark with a chuckle. They all had a laugh, except Nancy. Sonya completed the short drive to the hospital and pulled the car into the emergency room parking lot, where they were met by a team of Tupelo policemen and medical attendants.

Rose had already been rushed to the operating room, where her punctured right lung was repaired, and her spleen was removed. She was still in remarkably good shape for a woman of her age and was expected to make a full recovery. The doctor came out of the OR and counseled Clark concerning the surgery and estimated recovery time. Clark prepared to have Rose guarded by the Tupelo police while she was recovering from surgery and then planned to have her brought to his compound. Once again, Clark had missed total disaster and been rescued by his friends. Maybe the Lord really did look after drunks and fools.

After the doctor's report on Rose, Nancy asked Kirk and Sonya to go to the hospital cafeteria and buy them all a coffee. After they left, she asked the Tupelo police detail to move to the hall so she and Clark could have some privacy. Nancy sat up straight, threw her shoulders back, and spoke directly to Clark, "Clark Johnson, you know I love you like a brother, and I am your Christian sister, but I am getting too old for your shenanigans. You are an amazing leader that has altered the world we live in, but you could be the most selfish man I have ever known."

Clark interrupted, "Aw, Nan, you're not old—I'll bet you could run a marathon tomorrow if—"

"Don't try and change the subject, Clark. This is not a negotiation! If Isaac hadn't told Julianne where you were, and my strike team hadn't arrived just in the nick of time, you and Rose would be dead now!"

"Yes, ma'am, I'm sorry. Uh, please go on."

"Clark, you are going to change, or I am going to resign my position on the RBMT and retire from the Navy. Do you understand me? And don't give me that 'whipped puppy' look—I am serious! Now, I've got to start investigating to find out who was responsible for this attack."

Clark didn't say a word but looked at his feet as Nancy rose and silently walked out of the hospital room. Kirk and Sonya passed her in the hall, and Nancy simply stared straight ahead while ignoring them. Kirk said in a whisper, "Wow! Did you see that fierce look on Admiral Choi's face? Have you ever seen her like that before? What do you think is going on?"

"I've definitely seen that look before, Kirk—it means that somebody just got a good old-fashioned chewing."

CHAPTER 23

Back to Work

Clark had Isaac's car towed back to Texas, and he traveled back with Nancy, Kirk, and Sonya by private jet. Nancy seemed back to her old self, but Clark knew that her threats of resignation were serious. Clark turned his phone back on and discovered 106 calls with thirty-seven voice mails. Twenty-two of the voice mails were from Julianne, and Clark knew he had to call her even if she had been notified that he was all right. Clark dialed the number, and she answered without saying hello, "Daddy! Do you know how frightened I've been?" There was a long pause, and then the "Julianne tears" started. A little weeping at first turned into a torrent of sobs.

"Julianne, sweetheart, I am so sorry. Running off like that was such a foolish and insensitive thing for me to do. I was just so frustrated in trying to deal with that bullheaded ultra-liberal husband of yours that I just had to get away and clear my head, so..."

"Daddy, if you think for one minute that I am gonna listen to you blame Seth for your own stupid actions, then we'll just hang up now!"

"I didn't mean that like it came out, sweetheart. Seth's a good man and a tough negotiator, but you are right; my actions are my actions and nobody else's. I have always tried to blame someone or something else for my mistakes, but that is not the way to live. It makes people mad, and God doesn't like it either!" Clark said with a chuckle.

"Okay, Daddy, I forgive you, but Little Clark is crying, and I have to go. C'ya when you get home."

Clark hung up from his conversation with Julianne and laid his head back on the smooth leather seat headrest. After just a few seconds, he was asleep.

*****

Dr. Amanda Adams was the forensic analysis expert and leader of the team Nancy used in most of her investigations. Amanda had been pouring over the evidence from the assassination attempt on Clark. The bodies of the slain assassins had been gathered for transfer to the local morgue, where Amanda would study them for evidence. However, one of the assassins was still alive but unconscious when the Tupelo coroner's office arrived to remove the bodies. He was immediately transferred to the local hospital and stabilized before surgery to remove three armor-piercing bullets from his gut.

Amanda had already identified the grenade as an older model used by the American military during the Iraq war in the 1990s. The rifles the men carried and even the body armor were from that same time period and could be purchased at any military salvage store. When Amanda found out that the assassin who lived had survived the surgery, she notified Nancy.

The lone living assassin was none other than Ethan James, the leader of the Misfits. He had been awake about a day when Nancy and her bodyguards strode into his hospital room. "Hello, Admiral Choi. How ya been?" Ethan said weakly as he nodded in the direction of Sonya and Kirk.

"Ethan, I am utterly amazed. I would expect something like this from my rat of a half-sister Angel Jack, but you are way too smart to try an assassination attempt in broad daylight."

"I wanted to wait until nightfall, but my contact inside the RBMT security squad told me that Isaac had spilled the beans to Julianne, and I knew you would be here pronto."

"So, who is your contact, and why did you try to kill Clark?"

"I have been paying a woman named Tiffany Gordon, who works as Isaac's administrative assistant, for information on Clark and Seth's movements. The purpose of the kill was to stop the formation of a New USA. We Misfits were happy with the old USA, flaws and all. The plan was to kill either Seth or Clark. It didn't matter which one. Either kill would have grounded the formation of a New USA to a halt. And don't bother looking for Tiffany. She probably ran off to Mexico by now."

*****

Seth had asked Clark to stop by his office Monday morning before the next round of constitutional talks began. Clark strode into Seth's office, and Seth gave him a big hug. Clark was puzzled because Seth was not the hugging type.

"Clark, I am so sorry for the pressure I've put on you during the constitutional negotiations. Plus, it's hard enough to discuss these issues with lawyers from both sides jumping up to object on the basis of their interpretation of what's being discussed. So, I did us both a favor and told the lawyers to stay out of the meetings. No one will be there but you, me, and the lawmakers. The lawyers can review our final rough draft."

"Seth, I think that's a wonderful idea. James Madison, one of the Founding Fathers, wrote the document that formed the basis for the original constitution. Then, the state constitutional convention members 'tweaked' Madison's work to come up with a finished document. How about you and I write a constitutional document that is based on the original U. S. Constitution but contains compromises that will please both of our constituent groups? We can then let the lawmakers examine it and recommend changes before the lawyers ever see it. It's been my experience that many people tend to offer input in order to justify their existence rather than make a project better."

Seth chuckled and said, "I never thought of it that way before, Clark, but I believe you are right. Everybody wants to be significant, and sometimes, as people chase their own worthiness, they create work for the rest of us."

"So, let's make a big pot of coffee and get started," said Clark in his prominent Southern accent. The men withdrew to Clark's plush apartment/office and seated themselves across from each other with their laptops ready to go.

"What's the number one Red Nation policy that you hate the most, Seth?" asked Clark.

"Well, there are so many of your policies that I hate; it's hard to pick just one!" chuckled Seth. "If I have to pick one...it's got to be capital punishment. Your public hangings for major offenses will forever be a blight on this land!" said Seth sharply as he looked directly into Clark's eyes.

Clark ignored the harsh response and said, "I hate the Blue policies too, but my single most despised Blue

Nation policy is abortion on demand! How can you take me to task on capital punishment, which is a biblical concept, when you stand in agreement with the murder of over 300,000 unborn Blue Nation babies through abortion every year! Plus, 92 percent of the babies who are killed by abortion are only destroyed for birth control measures!" exclaimed Clark in his best preacher's voice.

"Now, you've gone too far, preacher man!" Seth shouted while rising to his feet and towering over Clark.

Just as Clark was standing up to respond, the door flew open, and an incredibly angry Julianne appeared holding Little Clark. As soon as Little Clark saw his daddy screaming at his granddaddy, he began to wail pitifully.

Julianne's eyes were swollen and red from crying, but she spoke firmly, "Seth, do you want to see your child and wife again? How about you, Daddy, would you like Little Clark and me out of your life?"

"Now, just a minute Julianne, can't we discuss this like reasonable adults?" Seth said rather firmly.

"I would be glad to do that if I were married to a reasonable adult! But I'm married to a bully, and my daddy ran away from his responsibilities and almost got assassinated. I have had it with you two! Either you work together to put this country back together, or I'm gone!"

"Come on now, Julianne, where would you go?" asked Clark in a mellow voice.

"Don't worry about that, Daddy. It's all set up. I have a luxury apartment with room for two female security guards, and I paid for it with *your money*. Plus, I have several of these shouting matches of yours on tape, and I will not hesitate to share them with both nations. You 'schoolyard boys' have exactly one hour to give me your decision. I'll either leave or stay—it's your choice. Are you going to lay down your pride and work together, or not?" Julianne then whirled around while still holding the now screaming Little Clark and walked out the door.

CHAPTER 24

Back to Work 2.0

"That was one mad woman!" Seth exclaimed.

"That was one hurt woman, too," added Clark.

"And we are the reason," said Seth slowly.

The two men decided to call it a night after Seth called Julianne and put her on speaker phone where they could both apologize. Julianne accepted their apology but told them in no uncertain terms that they must follow through with their promises or she would carry out her threat to leave them both.

Seth and Clark met for coffee at 7 a.m. the next day before going back to the conference room to get to the task of recrafting a new constitution that would be acceptable to the lawmakers, lawyers, and 75 percent of the populace of each nation. Even though both nations were designed to be democracies rather than constitutional republics, it took a super majority of 75 percent of the people to ratify any new laws or especially a new constitution for the New United States of America.

A sleepy-eyed Clark sipped his mocha latte and asked quietly, "So, how did it go with Julianne last night, my friend?"

"It didn't. She was locked in our suite when I arrived and failed to respond when I gently knocked on the door. She has everything she needs to stay secluded as long as she wants. I know she has forgiven me in principle, but I sure would like to see her beautiful smile."

"Don't worry, Seth. She will come around. She's a lot like her mother. Heck, I got locked out of the bedroom three weeks after the honeymoon!"

They both chuckled softly and then walked to the conference room, where they were met by their personal administrative assistants and a computerized stenographer. Seth suggested they go back to the ideas that caused the big blow-up a few days ago.

Clark agreed and went to his line of questioning from a few days ago.

"Okay, we've already established that the law you hate the most is capital punishment, and we Reds hate abortion being used as a means of birth control. Now, let's not argue our points again but ask the question, how can we compromise on this issue? Let's try and solve one issue and then go on to others."

"This is a tough one for me because a woman deserves to have the right to—"

"Don't start, Seth...we are not going to argue!"

"Let's choose another area then. How about...disparity in earning power for marginalized minority citizens?" asked Seth.

"That's a good issue, my friend, but it's not a constitutional question. Please give me your thoughts on something from the original documents."

While Seth and Clark brainstormed in a reasonable manner, Nancy was just getting to her office in the compound. As she strode into the foyer adjacent to her office area with companions Kirk and Sonya, she was quickly approached by her chief aid, Amber Glass. Amber had a worried look on her usually cheery face as she handed Nancy a crystal memory drive.

"Good morning, Admiral. I opened your inner office this morning to prepare for your arrival and found this crystal memory drive sitting right in the middle of your desk. I scanned it for malware, viruses, and even physical toxins, and it's clean, but...it's from Angel Jack!"

"Angel Jack! How can you be sure?"

"Somehow, she had it placed in your office and hacked into our communication system, leaving a message saying it had been delivered. The message also said your thumb print would activate the drive."

"She could have lifted my thumbprint from one of our encounters, but she had to have help getting it into my office," mused Admiral Choi.

"This could be very dangerous, ma'am," said Amber in a whisper.

"That's okay, Amber. If you checked it out and believe it's clean, then it's clean."

Nancy took the crystal memory drive back into her office and set it in the drive pocket. While Kirk and Sonya looked on, she placed her thumb on the top of the drive. Almost instantaneously, the drive shed a soft blue light and whirred for a second or two before projecting a visual holographic image of Angel Jack's face into the space above the desk.

"Hello, big sister. Thank you for taking the time to open my message. Let me get right to the point. I would like to meet with you. No guns, no knives, no bodyguards, no phones. Just you and me, face to face."

Nancy was shaken. Was this really the woman who hated her and had tried to kill her on numerous occasions? Nancy continued watching the hologram.

"If you are willing to meet, I will send you the coordinates of an out-of-the-way place outside Dallas that can accommodate your jet-copter."

Nancy was baffled but curious. Why would Angel Jack want to meet and talk, almost like a couple of sisters getting together?

"Don't do it, Stretch!" said Sonya in almost a shout. Kirk gave the idea a "thumbs down" sign and quickly agreed with Sonya.

"Thanks for your concern, but let me think about it. I'm going to the executive gym and work out. I will see you two after lunch," said Nancy as she quickly turned and walked out of her office.

CHAPTER 25

The Founding Fathers Were Brilliant!

"It's hard to believe that a bunch of old guys wearing white wigs and knickers crafted such an amazing document," muttered Seth.

"They also believed they had divine guidance to go along with their keen intellects," stated Clark.

"Let's not have the 'deity discussion' today, Clark. Let's agree that the original document governed this country nicely for over 260 years until our ill-advised coup destroyed it."

"I agree. Let's go back to the task at hand and come up with a constitution that will unite our two countries. As a matter of fact, I have a proposition for you that could solve a lot of the animosity between Blues and Reds over the last few decades," said Clark.

"Okay, I'm listening," sighed Seth.

"Originally, the Electoral College provided the Constitutional Convention with a compromise between two main proposals: the popular election of the president and the election of the president by Congress. You liberals despise the Electoral College on several fronts but mainly have wanted to abolish it in favor of a simple majority of votes. The conservatives, on the other hand, feel that if the Electoral College is abolished, the country will be run by the large population centers on the East Coast and West Coast. Am I right so far, Seth?"

"You simplified it as you do with most things, but that's basically correct."

Clark ignored the obvious "dig" and continued, "In the last presidential election that put Kennedy Watson into office, only 19 percent of American counties voted for Watson, but he won the popular vote handily. This difference clearly shows us why rural America, and conservatives in general, have felt disenfranchised for decades. Why don't we figure out a way to include local politics (the counties) and the Electoral College in the election process while giving more weight to the popular vote?"

"Actually, Clark, that seems reasonable," said Seth through a chuckle.

"So, as a starting point, we'll weigh all three equally. Our lawmakers can crunch the numbers and come up with a workable and fair equation," said Clark. Seth nodded in agreement.

The fact that Clark and Seth actually agreed on something was encouraging to both of them and the skeleton staff that was working with them. Two of their administrative assistants stood and cheered, and the whole room broke into laughter.

Over the next couple of months and after hours of debate, Charles and Seth wrote down tentative changes or modifications to the original constitution that were all based on compromise. Here are five of the basic changes that were presented to the lawmakers and constitutional lawyers:

1. All elected officials will have term limits. The president and vice president can serve two terms of four years each. The senators can serve up to two terms of four years each, while the House of Representative members can serve four terms of two years. All federal judges, including the Supreme Court, would be limited to twelve years of service on a specific court or a retirement age of seventy-two. The states that ratified the agreement would also have to agree to similar term limits for their state officials.

2. The death penalty would be abolished in the entire New USA.

3. Abortion restriction would be regulated by the states as it had been in the old USA after Roe v.

Wade was overturned by the Supreme Court in the 2020s.

4. The New USA and all of its states would agree to a balanced budget over a three-year period. The three-year period, rather than a yearly balancing of the budget, allows for extra expenditures during emergency situations.

5. All education above high school would be paid for by the government, provided the students maintained their grades and gave a year of service to the less fortunate through *The Peace Corp*, military service, or approved non-profit organizations that reached out to the poor. Handicapped students would work as support staff.

6. New bills would be created by the legislative branch but would have to receive a 75 percent favorable national vote from the whole populace before becoming actual law.

After three additional months of tweaking by the lawmakers and constitutional lawyers, these changes and many others were drafted into a New USA Constitution and sent to the states for ratification. The states were given six months to ratify the constitution and join the new union. All the states were on board with the New USA except for Texas, California, Oregon, and Washington. The three West Coast states combined to form a new country called Progressive States United (PSU). Texas thought the new constitution was too liberal and formed the Republic of Texas.

Both the Republic of Texas and PSU would rely on and make payments to the New USA for military protection. The two new countries would be treated like Canada or Mexico in trade and other business dealings.

It would take an additional eighteen months to hold federal elections and reestablish the old workings of the federal government, but the New USA was becoming a reality.

CHAPTER 26

The Sisters

Nancy, Kirk, and Sonya made small talk in the back of the jet-copter as the pilot made his way toward the coordinates that Angel Jack had supplied. The location was about forty miles West of Dallas in a rural region close to the Pecan Hill area.

"Admiral Choi, are you *really* not going to take a weapon to this meeting with the world's worst assassin?" asked Kirk.

"No, I'm not. Angel Jack is a lot of things, but she has never lied to me."

"Right, she will tell you the absolute truth while she's sticking that stiletto between your ribs," said Sonya sarcastically.

"I know you two love me and are concerned about this meeting, but there is a different feeling about this contact with my half-sister."

"We do love you, Stretch, and we'll be monitoring your meeting using the Alpha I Spy Satellite. The Alpha I system will be able to develop real-time images of you and Angel Jack using its optical vision to trace your infrared heat signatures. The images will be sent instantaneously to our position only ten miles away," said Sonya.

"But we couldn't reach you any quicker than about five minutes if you get into trouble," Kirk stated seriously.

The pilot banked sharply to the right as he saw the landing pad behind a house nestled in a pecan grove. As they got closer to the dwelling, Nancy could make out a small yellow cottage with white shutters and a black roof. The small backyard was enclosed by a white picket fence and what appeared to be a vegetable garden lay in neat rows just beyond the back screen porch.

The copter settled onto the landing pad, next to Angel Jack's own mini jet-copter. The pilot held the copter steady but active as he waited for Nancy to depart. When Nancy was safely out of the way of the circulating blades and jet thrusters, the pilot, Sonya, and Kirk lifted off and disappeared into the heavens. Nancy was now alone, with no weapons or means of communication.

Nancy passed the whole house generator with its huge propane tank and walked around to the front entrance, where she headed toward the freshly painted white front door. She took note of the immaculately appointed front porch with its beautiful white spindle railing, Shasta daisies in the flower boxes under the two windows, and beautiful red geraniums in planters on each side of the door. Nancy ascended the stairs, stepped onto the brightly colored welcome mat, and gently rapped on the door. A husky female voice said, "Come in," and Nancy slowly turned the knob and opened the door.

She was totally unprepared for what she saw. Angel Jack was seated on a beautiful brocade French-style sofa and was wearing a strapless yellow sundress and simple leather sandals. Her long blonde hair cascaded over her tan shoulders and accentuated her high cheekbones. The finishing touch to her appearance was her perfectly manicured nails that had been painted a soft apricot color. She looked like she had just stepped out of a glamour magazine except for the 9mm pistol she was holding with its barrel buried inside her mouth.

Angel Jack removed the pistol long enough to say, "So, big sister, how do you like my little hideaway?" Then she smiled sweetly before reinserting the pistol between her perfectly painted lips.

Nancy's heart was racing, but her SEAL training had taught her not to show emotion in the face of certain danger or surprise situations. "Gee, I think it's swell, sis," said Nancy as her eyes darted around the flawlessly decorated room. She was taken back by the mannequins of a man, two children, a cat, and a dog that were sitting in the room, but she fought the urge to show surprise.

Angel Jack took the pistol out of her mouth and said pleasantly, "Let me introduce you to my family. My husband Ken is an engineer on an offshore drilling rig. He works five days on and three days off, but the company picks him up and copters him out to the rig. I miss him when he's gone, but he is always home for dinner on his first day back. My children are Buck and Lucille. They are such good kids, and it's a pleasure to home-school them. Ollie, our dog, is a seven-year-old golden retriever who is incredibly playful and totally housebroken. The Siamese cat you see curled up on the hearth is named Bear. He is super affectionate when awake, but he sleeps much of the time. We're just one big happy family, sis!"

Nancy nodded in the direction of the mannequin husband, who was sitting in a recliner reading a book, and the two children, who had smiles frozen on their faces as they played the old board game Monopoly. She then realized that the dog and cat were not dolls but were actually real animals stuffed by a taxidermist. Who would stuff their own pets? Nancy could feel a little nausea exiting her stomach and rising toward her mouth. She turned away momentarily as if to clear her throat but actually bit her lower lip hard to allow the pain to help her refocus.

"Your family and home seem very nice, Angelica, but I thought we agreed on no weapons for our meeting," said Nancy.

"Of course, we did, sis. Don't be confused by this training gun. It certainly looks real, but it's not. I just keep it around to practice actually blowing my head off when the time comes."

Angel Jack put the training gun on the coffee table and said, "I have some tea brewing. Please take a seat, and I'll go fetch it."

Nancy sat in a Queen Ann armchair covered in deep red velvet upholstery and let out a stress-relieving sigh. *What was this all about?* she pondered.

Angel Jack came back in a few minutes with a silver serving tray containing a pot of tea, two teacups and saucers, and several types of sweeteners and cream. She set the tray on the coffee table and seated herself back on the couch. She had changed into a pair of khakis, a black tee-shirt, and black sneakers. Plus, she had removed the blonde wig and sported her own short brown hair. Angel Jack poured two cups of tea, and Nancy put one cube of sugar into her cup, stirred, and took a sip. The tea tasted normal. Nancy figured that she would already be dead if Angel Jack wanted her that way.

"Okay, Angelica, what's with the beautiful furniture, the mannequins, and the fancy clothes? And why are we meeting anyway?" asked Nancy.

Angel Jack took a sip of her tea, looked Nancy straight in the eyes, and began, "We both know that I am a wanted fugitive, and some say the world's greatest assassin. However, I really never wanted to hurt anyone; I just wanted to have a family and be normal. After my parents disowned me and kicked me out of the house, I lived in my martial arts instructor's dojo for a while and then joined a gang. The gang gave me a type of family and an opportunity to lead. We were making money off prostitution and drugs, and I was in charge of training new recruits in fighting and weapons techniques. We lived in a big house together, and I had my own room. Everything was great until we got busted by the FBI. In lieu of jail time, I agreed to work for them. The jobs were easy at first, mainly undercover work in other cities. But one day, my handler picked me up and took me to a meeting with his boss, Special Agent Dorsey. Agent Dorsey got straight to the point and offered me $20,000 plus expenses to kill a Chinese national that was spying on a nuclear research project in Northern California. They gave me $10,000 upfront and told me I would get the rest of the money when the job was done. I relocated to that area and began to work in the same research facility as my target. I caught him working late one night and strangled him with a length of piano wire. It was easy."

"Wait a minute, the FBI made you into an assassin?" said an incredulous Nancy.

"Yes, they did, and I became good at it. They sent me after higher valued targets and raised my pay to $100,000 a hit. In fact, I was famous in the agency. They called me the BOG or Black Ops Girl. As things progressed, I decided to go out on my own. I had saved plenty of money and simply stole my assigned jet-copter, removed all tracking devices, and left the area. I burned off my fingerprints with acid and changed my name to Angel Jack. The rest is history. As for this place and the mannequins, this is my adult dollhouse. When I was a little girl, a kind lady from a church around the corner gave me a yellow dollhouse at Christmas time. I kept it hidden in my room and would play with it when my father wasn't around and dream about a family of my own. I was able to hide it for about six months before he found it and broke it into pieces. But he can't break this full-sized one. It is mine!"

"Angelica, I am so sorry for all you've been through. It is truly terrible, but I have to ask you why you wanted to meet with me?" queried Nancy.

"Well, Nan, I've been surveilling you for a while now, and I have to say that I've seen a change in your life, your attitudes, and even your countenance. I figured you were just like me, except you worked for the government and not for yourself. I even saw you going to Bible studies of all things. Would you please tell me what has changed you? Maybe there's hope for me."

Nancy sat in stunned silence for a moment and then began, "Jesus changed me, Angelica. He is real, and His Spirit now lives in me and guides me in all I do. I am genuinely at peace for the first time in my life."

At first, Angelica just stared at Nancy, and then she looked away. Tears began to flow in a trickle that quickly became a deluge. Angelica fell on the floor in front of Nancy and placed her head in Nancy's lap. She sobbed for a few minutes before composing herself and asked Nancy in a whisper, "Do you think He could change me too?"

By now, Nancy was also weeping and said through her tears, "Oh, Angelica, I know He would! He has already died for all your sins. You just have to ask Him to forgive you and make Him the Lord of your life."

"But I've murdered whole families! I've gotten over thirty kills to my name...He wouldn't help the likes of me..."

"Let me tell you a story, Angelica. There once was a man named Saul who hated Jesus and all of His followers. Saul was vicious and cruel. He would ransack churches and have all the believers thrown into horrible dungeons where many of them died. One day, Jesus appeared to Saul as he was traveling to the town of Damascus. After Saul came face to face with Jesus, he turned away from his sins and began to preach the same gospel that he once despised. Saul eventually became the apostle Paul, who wrote over half the books in the New Testament. If Jesus would change that guy, He would surely accept and change you. He loves you and is calling you to a new life, Angelica."

Angelica remained silent for a few moments and then dried her tears, rose from the floor, and walked toward the back of the house. She appeared in a few minutes, wearing her flight suit and carrying a duffle bag. She hugged Nancy tightly and said, "I'm sorry, sis, but I can't do it." Then Angel Jack walked out the door, climbed into the cockpit of her mini jet-copter, and slowly rose into the sky before engaging the jet thruster.

Nancy sat motionless and silent as she pondered the past half-hour of interaction with her sister. The cottage, the make-believe family, the character changes, the revelation of stalking, the history of Angel Jack's evolution into the world's worst assassin, the cry for help, and the rejection of the one who could help, had Nancy numb and in shock. Her pulse raced, her vision was still clouded with warm tears, and movement seemed impossible. From the depth of her soul, Nancy whispered, "Please don't give up on her, Lord."

CHAPTER 27

Reunion!

The political landscape had changed significantly with the ratification of the new constitution and formula that calculated the victors of the various political offices. The Democrats and Republicans were still around, but term limits had decimated their idea of career politicians serving for decades in Washington, D. C. Plus, the libertarian party and various splinter groups ran candidates for office as well. Many of the old senators and representatives that had served for many years decided not to run and went back to their law practices or simply retired.

When the presidential votes were tallied using the new algorithmic formula that weighted the popular vote, the Electoral College, and the counties, Leon Brown and his vice-presidential candidate, who ran as socially conservative libertarians, only carried 40 percent of the vote and were forced into a runoff with the democrat candidate. The Republicans threw their support behind Leon, and after the votes were tallied, he won handily. Leon Brown would be the first president of the New USA.

The new landscape of the House of Representatives with less than 400 members and the Senate at 92 (due to the four states not rejoining the union) was extremely different from the one the Red Blue coup had removed. There were more business owners and religious leaders than there were lawyers. Three Misfits, running as libertarians, had been elected to the House of Representatives. The term limits seemed to be having the desired effect. Senators and congressmen would make their laws, send them to the populace for a 75 percent approval, serve their terms and then go home to live under the new laws they had created. Because of the 75 percent national approval requirement, only 15 percent of new laws passed anyway.

With Charles and Maria now married, the former prime ministers did not seek political office but joined Leon's new cabinet as his close personal advisors. Maria was still very liberal, and Charles was ultra-conservative, but their individual voices moved the whole administration toward moderation. The new vice president, James Thomas, who was one of the original lawmakers, became a valuable and wise asset to the presidential team.

When the states ratified the constitution, the USA was essentially a country again. A day of celebration had been planned for March 15 and was officially named Reunification Day. The New USA flag had been designed to closely emulate the old flag, but it had a purple border framing the entire body of the flag. The purple was a blending of red and blue, and it bound the future and the past together in reunification. It was a reminder of the need to blend diverse ideologies together into unity. The purple would forever proclaim the great difference between unity and uniformity. There were only forty-six stars, but the thirteen stripes (seven red and six white) were still evident. Millions of new flags were produced well in advance of Reunification Day, and they were being flown everywhere.

All the news services carried the reunification ceremony from the original capital grounds. After the opening prayer, Seth and Charles spoke first and once again humbly asked the country to forgive them for using the threat of nuclear weapons as a means of seizing power. A local mayor, a police chief, a female marine sergeant, a schoolteacher, and a farming couple gave the main addresses, and they all stressed unity. The country had been dissolved, suffered through great discord, endured major catastrophes, and was now being reunited. It was a great day!

After the reunification celebration was over, the former Red Blue Team met for a final banquet with entertainment and dancing in the classic Jefferson Hotel.

They were all going their separate ways now. Seth, a very pregnant Julianne, and Little Clark were moving to New York City, where Seth would host a morning talk show. Clark had sold his compound and was moving his ministry out of the Republic of Texas to Atlanta, Georgia. With a much humbler spirit, he began to rebuild his business of saving souls and changing lives. Admiral Nancy Choi was going back to the Pentagon as head of the joint chiefs. Sonya and Kirk had officially left law enforcement and been assigned to Nancy's department as her special assistants.

As Clark danced with Julianne, he told her how proud he was that she was his daughter and thanked her once again for forgiving him for all the messes he had made.

"Aw, Daddy, you know I can't stay mad at you long, and I am very proud that I am your daughter," Julianne said with a giggle.

Maria and Charles held each other tightly as they swayed to the music while President Brown and his First Lady moved through the crowd shaking hands and hugging necks. Everyone promised to stay in touch, and Leon suggested they have a similar event every year on Reunification Day.

While the friends were saying their final goodbyes and the staff was clearing tables, no one noticed the assistant to the maître d'. She was a smartly dressed middle-aged woman with an athletic build and soft brown hair that fell just below her shoulders. When she reached out to make the final entry in the event book, her wrist extended just far enough from her black blazer that the tattooed initials "AJ" were clearly visible. No one was watching her, but she was carefully watching them.

A Note from the Authors

Thank you for reading our book. We hope you enjoyed it!

We realize that America is made up of people from different backgrounds, races, religions, economic layers, and political viewpoints, and we believe those differences should be celebrated. However, we also believe that a country must protect the rights of its citizens through a strong military and a free press. We believe in democracy but also believe that public servants should actually serve and be willing to work with those who hold different views.

These are the views of the authors, but your views may be totally different from ours. So, how would you make changes, if any, to our culture and possibly the constitution? Did you like the changes that Clark and Seth made to the election process, or would you keep things the way they currently are? What are your opinions and ideas?

Also, I'm sure you noticed that our story contains characters that are both believers and non-believers in Jesus. What are your thoughts about Jesus? Is He God's Son as He claimed to be? If you are interested in having a relationship with Jesus, simply go back and reread chapter 10, pages 112–117, where Kirk prays with Nancy and Sonya to receive Jesus as Lord. Just pretend you are sitting at the table with them, and Kirk is explaining the message of Jesus to you also.

Then simply pray the same prayer that Kirk prayed with Nancy and Sonya. If you prayed that prayer from your heart, then you are saved and part of the family of God! We encourage you to read the Bible and pray every day and find a church that will help you grow in your faith.

We would love to hear your thoughts concerning Red Nation Blue Nation, and be sure and let us know if you prayed to receive Jesus as Lord!

Please email us at *LarryAnn@RednationBluenation.com*
Blessings!
Larry and Ann Nunnally.

Endnotes

1 Psalm 51:10.
2 Exodus 20:13; Deuteronomy 5:17 (KJV).
3 1 Corinthians 11:24-25, 27-29.

CPSIA information can be obtained
at www.ICGtesting.com
Printed in the USA
LVHW081459020822
725009LV00013B/532